Omega's Br

Carter's Crossing: Book

MW01153357

Aiden Bates

© 2019

Disclaimer

Contents

Chapter 1

Royce

It wasn't every day that I had the honor of walking in on my boss bending my boyfriend over the executive table in the boardroom.

Thank god for little miracles, I guess. By age forty, I'd thought I'd be done with this crap.

It was hard to say how long I stood in the doorway, watching them go at it, but finally, I convinced myself that I had to say something. "Am I interrupting something? I can always grab lunch and come back later if you two need to, y'know. Finish up."

"Royce!" Brendan went white as he scrambled to pull his pants back up. It was no easy feat, since he still had Don's cock balls-deep inside him. "Honey, I—I came in to bring you…"

"The Keller report," Don said with a cough, finally pulling his dick out of my boyfriend's ass. "You, ah. Forgot it at home. Brendan here was just—"

"Making himself useful?" I eyed them both with my best do-I-look-stupid glare and held the thick file folder in my hand up for both of them to see. "Spare me the song and dance, guys. I've got the Keller report right here—and your lube is still on the table, for fuck's sake."

"Royce, babe. I can explain—" Brendan's belt clanged against the button of his jeans as he struggled to buckle it.

I shook my head. "Save it, Brendan. I think it's fair to say that this is where things end for us, don't you? Have a nice life."

"Royce, about all this—I can explain." Don removed the lube from the table in a single, fluid motion. I appreciated that about Don. Sure, I'd just caught him fucking my boyfriend, but at least he was keeping his composure about it.

"Looks pretty cut and dried to me. Or, uncut and well-lubed, so to speak." I made a point of not looking at Don's cock again as he tucked it back into his suit pants and tossed the Keller report down on the table. "Came in so you could debrief me on this, but it looks like you already gave Brendan here my debriefing for me."

"Royce, please!" Brendan stumbled forward, desperation twisting his pretty-boy, Ken-doll face. "Let's just talk about this, okay?"

"Nothing to talk about." I held Don's gaze, not even bothering to give Brendan another moment of my attention. He didn't deserve it. "Don, I think it's fair to say that I'll be taking my vacation time now. How much do you reckon I've got racked up?"

Don cleared his throat and nodded. "Very fair. I'd say you've got a month or so. At least."

"Make it two."

Don paused, lowered his gaze, and nodded again. "Done."

"Royce—don't leave! Please, we can work this out—I can be better! There's something I should tell you—don't go! Royce, please, don't—"

The only answer to Brendan's pleadings I could give him was the sound of the boardroom doors slamming behind me on my way out. It wasn't until I was in my Porsche and twenty miles down the road that I was able to process what had just happened—or where I was headed, for that matter.

Was I hurt? Sure. But I'd never been the type to whine and whinge about a breakup—especially not over someone like Brendan. He'd been a good lay, but a shitty boyfriend. The number of times he'd fucked me over with his erratic mood swings and immature dramatics was too high to even bother counting.

They said there was an omega for every alpha, but in my case, I was beginning to seriously doubt it. Too many of my boyfriends had turned out to be like Brendan—and by too many, really, I meant every damn one of them. Sex-crazed, self-important, and with attention spans that didn't reach far beyond the tips of their own cocks.

Of course, at least Rick had had the tact to cheat on me with a cocktail waiter at the company Christmas party instead of my own boss, and when Mitchell slept with that alpha drag queen on our anniversary, he'd just picked up his things from my place the next morning and walked out the door.

I didn't know why I'd ever dreamed of Brendan being different. Part of me figured it was just clinging to little fragments of hope. Hadn't we talked about starting a family just last week?

The fucker had even cooed and sucked his way into convincing me to go at him without a condom a couple of nights. There I'd been, thinking I might be a dad in nine months or so—now, all I was thinking about was getting myself to the clinic and making sure he hadn't given me the clap or some shit.

A few days later, with a bag packed and a clean bill of health, I was on the road and leaving New York City far behind. It would have been easier to fly back to my hometown, but I figured I needed the drive to clear my head.

Besides—there was something to be said for seeing that sign on the side of the road again. Carter's Crossing, Virginia, nestled snug in the forested hills of the Blue Ridge Mountains. Population: 1,200.

Now that I was home again for a few months, I supposed they could make it 1,201.

"Royce! Bring it in, buddy!" The second I pulled up, my brother Cam met me outside the brewery that had accidentally become his livelihood. "You've got no idea how glad I am to see you."

I laughed as Cam wrapped me up in a bear hug. "Only because you're hoping I'll figure out a better way to sell your new lager to hipsters, huh?"

Cam rolled his bottle-green eyes. He was an alpha too, but he'd gotten his eyes from our omega dad. "Man, now that Hank sold me his shares to this place and bailed, I think we're going to need a lot more than just hipsters buying it. Come on in—I'll give you a taste test of our first batch."

Big Hops Brewing Company had started out as a joke between Cam and Hank, back when they were crashing on my couches and doing their undergrads at Columbia Business. In the years since Cam had graduated, I'd seen it grow from a badly-drawn rabbit-shaped logo on a cocktail napkin into an actual, functional business.

Functional, but not profitable. Judging by the hopeful look on Cam's face as I sipped at his latest test batch, he needed this win even more than I'd imagined.

"How're the books looking?" I asked tentatively before I gave him my review.

"In the black, some days." Cam shrugged and ran his fingers through his dark brown hair. That, he'd gotten from our alpha dad. My own hair was a darker shade, like our omega dad's. "Then I pay all the bills for the month and we're in the red again. Hank was probably smart for skipping out when he did, huh?"

"Probably," I agreed, shaking my head and passing the taste-tester back to him. "This thing is too hoppy to be commercial, Cam. You ever think about sweetening it up and mellowing it out a little bit?"

Cam sighed. "Yeah, I know. A guy can dream though, right?" He tucked the glass back behind the bar as the front door swung open, letting a gust of cool autumn air inside. "Ha—speaking of sweetening…"

I turned to see a fresh-faced kid come through the door, holding up a paper bag with the Lonely Hearts Diner logo on it. The logo looked good—seemed like the Diner had updated it since I'd last been in town—but the guy holding it looked even better. Boyishly handsome, forest-green eyes, a trucker's cap turned backwards over a mop of thick chestnut hair, and a set of biceps he must have earned throwing weights around at the local gym.

If he hadn't been so damn wholesome looking, I would have said he was just my type.

"Royce, meet Patrick Murray." Cam introduced us as he dug into the contents of the bag from the Diner. "Patrick, this is my big brother Royce."

"Big is right." Patrick laughed a little as he looked me up and down. "Nice to meet you, Royce."

I hoped I didn't intimidate him as I shook his hand. I was 6'5" even out of my dress shoes, and had spent my fair share of time at the gym myself—so even for 6'1" lookers like Patrick, it happened pretty often. The fact that I had to have been at least fifteen years his senior didn't help much.

At forty, I knew what I wanted out of life, and for the most part, I knew how to get it. Unless it came to keeping a steady boyfriend who didn't fall onto the first wild cock he saw, but that was neither here nor there.

As for Patrick, he couldn't have been much older than twenty-five. He had a good handshake for his age, though, and instead of balking at my massiveness, he just gave me a coy little smile.

"Are all you Wheelers so damn good looking?" Patrick asked Cam with another laugh. "You told me you'd inherited all the looks in the family, you lying bastard."

"How else was I supposed to convince you to go out with me?" Cam gave Patrick a wild grin as he extracted a to-go carton of pie from the delivery bag. "I was afraid if you found out how pretty our sister was, you might decide you were straight."

"Not my thing. I'm an omega," Patrick explained, giving me a quick glance. "Somehow I don't think things with Dana and I would have worked out."

"Stop flirting with my brother, you little shit." Cam balled up a napkin from the to-go bag and tossed it at Patrick, missing by a country mile. "And before you go getting any ideas, Royce, Patrick is my ex, so you can put your dick away now."

"My dick wasn't out. Wouldn't dream of it," I assured Cam, holding my hands up in innocence.

Admittedly, though, dreaming of it was exactly what I'd been doing. Patrick had the kind of lips that a man like me couldn't quite help myself around—which, I supposed, was exactly the reason I kept falling into bed with flighty omega drama queens.

Those lips were absolutely made for sucking cock. Cam's taste in beer might have left a little to be desired, but his taste in men was as excellent as ever.

"We *barely* dated." Patrick apparently felt the need to clarify Cam's announcement. Maybe it was just wishful thinking, but it seemed like he had been just thinking the same thing about *my* mouth. "But please, don't let me ruin your family reunion. Dana back in town too?"

"Rethinking switching teams, now that my bother's off limits?" Cam teased, balancing a huge mouthful of the diner's pie on a plastic fork. "Nah—she's still in the big city playing lawyer, I'm afraid."

"Shame," Patrick said with a laugh. "If the Wheeler boys are back in town with no one to keep them in line, I reckon we're all in trouble."

"Keep hanging around here, and you might be—hey!" I furrowed my brow in Cam's direction as he threw another napkin at me. This time, it hit its mark, bouncing off my right pec and falling uselessly to the floor.

"If you're planning on hanging around here, bring more pie next time." Cam went after his tossed napkins, picking them up and throwing them in the trash. "And tell your dad I said hi!"

A pink tinge touched Patrick's ears as Cam implied he might have overstayed his welcome. "Right, yeah. I oughta get back to the diner. Nice meeting you, Royce."

I shook his hand again, holding on for a little longer this time. "Nice meeting you too, Patrick. Don't be a stranger."

A little smile played on Patrick's perfect lip. "I'll try not to be."

After Patrick had left again, I caught Cam glaring at me. "Don't play coy with me, Roy. I know exactly what you're thinking—and no. Not gonna happen." He raised an eyebrow, shrugged, and returned to his pie. "Not until you're done being on the rebound, at least."

"Who says I'm thinking about that? Or that I'm on the rebound, for that matter."

Cam rolled his eyes. "Like I couldn't smell the pheromones flying between you two. And after the thing with Brendan? Your status is Rebound City, population: you."

"It's nothing," I assured Cam. "Kid was just starstruck by my dashingly good looks and big-city charm. You'd do the same if you'd stop eating pie for lunch like a rogue toddler."

"Hey!" Cam complained as I snatched his fork out of his hand and took a mouthful.

"Good pie, though." I grabbed my bag and headed out the back door to the loft that Cam and Hank had built behind the brewery. "Mind if I dig through your marketing files? If your lager doesn't start tasting better, you're going to need all the marketing help you can get."

"As long as that's all you're digging through," Cam called after me. "My little black book is still off limits, man!"

We both laughed as I headed off to work, but despite my denial of my attraction to Patrick, I knew Cam was right. There was something there between Patrick and me—not that I was about to act on it. omegas were trouble—especially handsome young omegas like Patrick.

His flirtatious vibes were fun in the moment, but I'd been around the block enough times to know how those eventually played out. Once I got him into bed, things would quickly shift from a sizzle into a slump. With him being Cam's ex and all … it just wasn't worth it. *He* wasn't worth it.

At least, that's what I thought.

Chapter 2

Patrick

It never felt good to be caught flirting, especially not by my own ex. The fact that I'd been caught flirting with my ex's older brother?

"I'm Patrick, I'm an omega. Why don't you just shut your pretty mouth and put a baby in me already, Royce?" I scoffed at my own idiot words as I slammed the door to my truck and headed back into the diner. At this rate, I'd never be able to go back to Big Hops ever again.

Cam had already made it clear that me gawking around at his older brother was a hard no, and in his defense, he'd had every right to. There weren't a lot of things more awkward than chasing after an ex's sibling—and with the way I'd been looking at Royce, my infatuation must have been written all over my face.

If there were rules here, I didn't even know what they might be. Cam and I had never gotten past a little heavy petting here and there in the romance department—but that didn't exactly mean that Royce was free game, either.

In my defense, though, Cam should have warned me that his brother was coming to town—and he definitely should have warned me that Royce looked like *that*. Everything I'd ever liked about Cam, I saw reflected in Royce—except Royce had those mysterious amber eyes and that city-boy charm to further lower my defenses and assist me in making an ass out of myself.

Well … city boy, not so much. City *man* would have been a little more accurate. Royce was all man, from his sleek leather boots to the way his massive shoulders filled out his white button-down. I'd never seen five o'clock shadow look so good on someone at eleven in the morning before—not that it mattered.

Like Cam had said, Royce was off limits—and like Royce had said, he wasn't interested, anyway.

"How's Cam doing?" Dad asked as I swung by the register and added Cam's lunchtime pie to his tab.

"Good. His brother's in town. Looks like they're trying to save the brewery with some clever marketing. He liked the pie."

Dad chuckled. "That boy and his pie. He'll figure the brewery thing out eventually. When your dad and I opened this place…"

Suddenly, Dad got quiet and turned his attention back to the soda he was filling. "It's a lot of work, owning a business. Good thing it's in your blood, huh?"

The Lonely Hearts Diner buzzed with lunchtime activity as Dad headed off to deliver the drinks to table six. It was a good sign, since we were almost always closed for dinner these days. My omega dad had always had a good head for keeping the books, but it had been my alpha dad who'd excelled at putting in the muscle to actually make the place work.

It still made my heart ache to see him struggling on with the place alone. It was obviously a two-man job, and as much as I tried to help out, I felt my alpha dad's absence in the diner as much as my omega dad did. Sometimes I wished that I was old enough to remember the diner's glory days. Maybe it would've made inheriting the place feel a little more right.

"Mind if I knock off?" I asked, as the last of the lunch rush trickled out the door.

"Sure you wanna go? I was thinking we could go over the books one more time before I close up for the day."

I laughed, closing out the till and hanging up my apron on the hook behind the front counter. "Dad, I know the books better than you do at this point."

Dad beamed with pride. "S'pose you're right. Okay, head on out, then. I assume you and Thomas have plans you'd like to get to. That carnival still in town?"

"Yeah, but I doubt we'll get much further than drinks out at Big Mike's," I assured him.

"Want me to let Rich and Peter's boy know you'll be out? He's got a nice new truck, you know. Shiniest chrome in the county. Bet he'd like to drive you home."

"Thanks, dad—but no thanks. Tom and I will split a cab home, and I'll be in first thing in the morning to check up on the vegetable delivery."

Dad got a little quiet again. I could tell he was fretting—and I knew exactly what he was fretting about. "Just be careful on the roads after dark, okay? Remember to warn the cab driver about honking when he goes around Devil's Bend."

I clapped Dad on the shoulder reassuringly. The thought of anyone taking Devil's Bend home at night still set his nerves off to this day. "I always do. I'll be careful, though, I promise."

"Love you, Son."

"Love you too, Dad."

Big Mike's was only a short walk from the Diner. It was the only gay bar in Carter's Crossing, but it was the only gay bar we needed. Big Mike maintained a dive-y enough atmosphere that it drew in plenty of alphas, and he usually had a drink special or two posted to ensure that there were plenty of omegas around to keep the place interesting.

"So, how was work? Your dad still hinting that he wants you to take over the diner?" Thomas asked, winking at Big Mike behind the bar and collecting our cocktails.

Big Mike winked back—he always did. Sometimes I wondered if he and Thomas had a thing going, but if it was true, then Thomas was doing a good job of hiding it.

"More than hinting," I groaned as we slid into our normal booth. "Last night he made me look at retirement villages with him. They all look like swingers' resorts, too."

"Figures," Tom said with an eye roll. "Your dad's going to be down in Florida, drowning in horny old alpha dick, and we're going to be stuck here with these clowns."

We eyed the group of alphas clinking beers and cracking billiards balls together across the room and sighed into our drinks simultaneously. Tom and I had tried our hand at most of the alphas in Carter's Crossing at this point—to no avail.

If I were honest with myself, Royce Wheeler was the most interesting prospect I'd had for a good date in months—so of course, he had to be out of bounds and out of my league. I considered telling Tom about him for a second, then thought better of it. If I wasn't allowed to throw myself at Royce, Tom sure as hell wasn't either.

"Let's not talk about my dad drowning in anything," I groaned. "Least of all horny old alpha dick."

"Fair. You could just tell him that you don't want to take over the diner, though, you know. Might solve a lot of your problems," Tom pointed out.

It was a good point, but not a useful one. "My dads built that place together. If I don't take it over, he'll either have to keep working there for the rest of his life or he'll have to sell."

"Maybe selling would be in his best interest, though. Help him, y'know. Let go of the past and everything."

I took a long sip of my drink and shook my head slowly. "I don't think he wants to let go of the past."

"If he's looking at alpha-omega retirement villages, he might be."

"If you don't pick an alpha and stick with him soon, *you're* going to be looking at alpha-omega retirement villages," I countered.

Tom pouted prettily. "But playing the field is so much more fun."

At that, it was my turn to roll my eyes. "I'm reminding you that you said that the next time I hear you bemoaning the lack of a ring on your finger."

"I don't bemoan!" Tom protested—but with little more than a glance of disbelief from me, he relented. "Okay, okay. But if you were in my shoes, you'd be annoyed too.

"I'm always planning all these gorgeous dream weddings for all these happy couples, dammit! And what do I get for my troubles? By the time the last dance is over, all I go home with is a sloppy make-out session with the least drunk of the groomsmen."

"And a paycheck," I reminded him. "Besides—you *do* get a lot of groomsmen."

Tom batted his eyelashes at me like Scarlett O'Hara at the Wilkes family barbecue and flicked the tip of my nose. "You'd get a lot of groomsmen, too, sweetheart—if you'd uncross your legs every once in a while. Or ever, for that matter."

I felt the pink rise up at the tips of my ears again. The subject of my virginity was something that Thomas never failed to bring up when we talked about our love lives—and it never failed to make me uncomfortable, either.

It wasn't like I didn't *want* to get laid. Every month, when I went into heat, I was practically begging to have a nice, hard cock in my ass, and a flood of cum flowing from the tip of it, too.

"Can we buy you boys a couple drinks?" a gruff voice asked as I stirred my Mai Tai with its little yellow umbrella.

Tom and I gave a quick up and down to the two alphas who'd just appeared at our table. Tall, handsome, well-dressed and reeking of cologne, they were obviously out-of-towners—but they lacked the elegance of Cam's handsome brother, and the way they were leering at us suggested that if I wanted to give my virginity up to either of them, I'd probably never hear from them again.

"No, thanks," I said with an apologetic smile, even as Tom kicked me under the table for it. "We're still working on these."

"Maybe another time, then." The taller of the two alphas gave me a smarmy grin and pointed to a table across the room. "You slutty little omegas change your minds, you know where to find us."

"That so?" Tom snapped back at the men. "Why don't you asshole alphas learn a set of manners or two before I call your daddies and let them know what arrogant pigs they raised, hmm?"

Grumbling, the alphas glared daggers at Tom and me as they made their way back to their tables. Tom bristled with indignation as they did it, but the whole encounter had left not just my ears, but my entire *face* red.

"Ugh," I groaned. "After that, I think I need a shower. Maybe I ought to go."

"Go? Now?" Tom looked at me like I'd sprouted a second head. "Honey, we've just arrived!"

"They called us *slutty*, dude. I'm not touching that kind of attitude with a ten-foot pole."

"Maybe if you'd loosen up a little, you'd find that you rather enjoy getting your ten-foot pole touched." Tom finished his drink, leaned back and gave me a petulant side-eye.

"Those two were assholes, sure—but come on, Pat. You don't want to work at your dad's diner. You don't want to fuck over-perfumed city slickers. What *do* you want?"

My mind wandered to the pile of unfinished sketches that I was stashing beneath the vegetable order forms in my office at the diner—then back to Royce Wheeler's scruffy, chiseled jawline and big, strong hands.

"Nothing that I'm allowed to have," I grumbled, finishing off my drink as well. "For now, I reckon another Mai Tai might do, though. Want me to go get us some refills?"

"And let you steal Big Mike from me? Don't make me turn you to chicken feed, Patrick." Thomas slid out of the booth and grabbed his coat. "Come on—I've just decided that we're entirely too pathetic together to sit here drinking all night."

I checked my watch. "Ready to head home already? It's only seven. Are you in heat or something? Got a booty call lined up?"

"Lord, I wish. But *no*, you nosy Nancy. I'm not horny, I'm *bored*. Carnival's in town. If we're going to ride this roller coaster of romantic despair again, we might as well do it on an actual roller coaster."

I cast a glance at the table of alphas again. To my disappointment, they caught me staring and raised their glasses to me—which made me look away immediately.

"Fine," I relented. "We'll go to your damn carnival. Just know that I'm only agreeing to this because I don't want those jackasses following us home."

"Worse things could happen," Tom said with a triumphant grin. "But I'll take it. It's about time we went out and had a little fun around here. See ya, Big Mike!"

Tom blew a kiss at the burly bartender, who caught it and tucked it into his pocket with a good-natured smile. For not the first time, I wondered what it would be like to have an alpha smile at me that—but I didn't have Tom's natural charisma, and I sure as hell couldn't think of any man in Carter's Crossing whom I'd actually want attention from.

Except, of course, for Royce Wheeler. Who was off limits. Just like my artistic notions—and any semblance of any other part of a life I might actually enjoy building for myself.

Fuck, I *was* getting mopey. Maybe Tom was right. I *did* need a little fun in my life—and fast, too.

Chapter 3

Royce

"That'll be five dollars, boys." Cam's glammed-up omega bartender, Nicky, purred at a couple of alphas as he handed them their beers. "Or, if you wanna take me out behind the beer tent and have your wicked ways with me, make it ten."

"It'll be five," I cut in with a growl. When Cam had asked me if I'd mind helping run the Big Hops beer tent at the Carter's Crossing carnival that night, I'd been all for it—but Nicky, in all his horniness and uselessness, was starting to grind on my nerves.

Typical omega nonsense. I was over it before it even started—and once it started, I would've done anything to end it. "We take cash, or cash."

Grumbling, the alphas paid up and wandered off to find entertainment elsewhere. Once they'd gone, Nicky turned to me with a glower.

"How the *hell* am I going to get knocked up if you keep scaring off the top draft picks, chief?"

I raised an eyebrow, crossing my arms over my chest. "Depends. Are you looking for a man, or are you looking for a football team?"

Nicky gave me a sultry smile and pressed up against me in a way that a less patient man than myself would have smacked him for. "Depends on who's asking, I guess. Are *you* interested in this hot 'n' ready man-womb, Roycey-poo?"

I looked down at him, unamused. "I'm going to tap another keg."

"Why tap those kegs when you could be tapping *this* keg, baby daddy?!" Nicky called after me with a cackle.

I didn't want to be the one to break it to him, but if that was his idea of flirtation, any genetic material that made it inside his "keg" would be from the bottom of the barrel. I had notoriously bad taste in omegas, and even *I* knew better than to go barking up that tree. Nicky was obviously in the mood, and while normally that would have tugged at my more basic instincts, I was finding myself perfectly unmoved by his humping-and-grinding antics.

If the mess with Brendan back in New York had taught me anything, it was that my omega-chasing ways weren't likely to net me anything close to actual, honest-to-god happiness. The fact that I'd almost been talked into having a baby with my loose-moraled ex was still weighing heavily on my mind—how badly I'd actually wanted it at the time, and how lucky I was that things had fallen apart before we'd actually gone through with it.

At least I could thank Cam for one thing that night, though. I'd figured that in the wake of my breakup, I'd at least want to find a quick, meaningless fuck to blow off some steam. But to my surprise, the urge just wasn't hitting me.

I didn't want a quick fuck—I wanted something more. Where I'd find it, I had no clue. It sure as hell wasn't up Nicky's horny omega ass, at least.

I hefted a keg off the truck and balanced it on my shoulder, hauling it across the tent with ease. In that, I guessed I had a second thing to thank Cam for. Lifting heavy shit and carrying it around was appealing to some macho-man set of neurons tucked away somewhere in the caveman part of my brain. I wouldn't have gotten the same satisfaction crunching and lifting my way to an eight-pack at the gym, that was for sure.

It felt good to be doing some*thing* rather than some*one* for once. Maybe Cam had known what he was doing when he'd asked me to work this shift for him after all.

No sooner had I gotten the keg tapped than I felt my phone start buzzing away in my pocket. It surprised me that I was even getting a signal out in Carter's Crossing, let alone that anyone was actually bothering to call me.

When I looked at the name on my caller ID, though, I could only groan with disappointment.

"Not a great time, Brendan." I didn't bother with a *hello* or a *how are you*. Brendan would have just seen it as an in—and as far as I was concerned, he was out of my life for good.

"Never is for you, huh?" Brendan's voice dripped with malice on the other end of the line. "Maybe if you'd been a little better at managing how you spend all that time of yours, I wouldn't have had to throw myself at your boss just to get laid."

I glanced at Nicky, who was watching with interest and doing his best to listen, then covered the mouthpiece of my phone. "Gotta take this. No freebies, no sucking, no fucking. Got it?"

Nicky pouted, sighing dramatically. "I'll try to control myself, chief."

I dismissed myself to the space out behind the beer garden, far enough away from the carnival that I could hear myself think and avoid being overheard.

"Look," I told Brendan. "I get it. You were unhappy with me for whatever reason—don't pretend like you weren't getting it on the regular, because we both know that's not true—so you fucked my boss. Explain to me why this is my problem now."

"You took off before I could grab my shit from your apartment, you asshole. And before you ask, *yes*, I tried to get in on my own, and *yes*, I'm very impressed with the tenacity of your doorman. The fucker even took my spare key. I hope you're proud of yourself."

Admittedly, I was more proud of Harry than I was of anything I'd done. The second I mentioned the incident to him, on my way out of town, he swore to me that he'd send Brendan packing on sight.

"Men like that cause problems, Roy. You just let me handle it, okay?" Harry'd told me.

It was good to know that I wouldn't be going home to a trashed apartment courtesy of my cheating ex, at least. *If* I went back to New York at all at this point—I was still figuring that out myself.

"What do you need, Brendan?" I asked tiredly—and immediately regretted it.

"I need you to *listen* to me, Royce! I need you to *forgive* me!"

"I meant from the apartment."

"Oh." There was a long pause, then Brendan sniffed indignantly. "My toothbrush, for one."

"Buy a new toothbrush."

"And I have *clothes* there, Royce! I have *things.* We were in the process of starting a family together, you asshole! At least tell Harry to let me in so I can pick up my birth control, for fuck's sake."

This conversation was starting to give me a headache—or maybe it was just the sound of Brendan's voice. Either way, I could hardly deny the man his birth control. Getting a refill would be an even bigger pain in the ass than taking my boss' dick, I reckoned—and as annoyed as I was with Don for fucking my boyfriend, I didn't think he'd be happy to find himself paying paternal support for Brendan's lovechild.

"Fine. Okay. Dana's still in the city. I'll text her, and she'll get you your stuff. Send me a list and she'll bring it by the bar tomorrow. You've got a shift, right?"

There was another long pause, then finally: "Yes. That's fine. But Royce—"

My eyes flicked back toward the beer tent, where Nicky was demonstrating to an alpha nearly three times his age how good he was at balancing plastic cups of beer on his ass.

"Gotta go. We're done here, yeah?"

"No, we are *not*—"

I hung up the phone before I had to listen to any more of Brendan's whining. It wasn't that I didn't think he had grievances to air—it was that I just didn't care anymore. I was doing my best to move on as quickly as possible. If he was smart, he'd do the same.

My only regret was that I hadn't told him to lose my number. But at least, once Dana got him his stuff, the emotional circus with Brendan would finally be over.

"No," I told Nicky definitively, grabbing the beer off his ass and handing it to the customer. "Bad."

"Spank me then, Daddy," Nicky cooed after me as I trudged through the crowd, typing out a text to Dana to let her know the situation.

I didn't exactly enjoy having to explain to my baby sister why she'd need to take time out of her busy day to cart a box of Brendan's things across Manhattan tomorrow. Even as I typed the message, I found myself getting more frustrated by the minute.

It was bad enough admitting that I'd managed to fall in bed with another cheating omega. It was becoming a running joke in my family that there must be something wrong with me to keep ending up in situations like this at my age, and I was fully expecting to get an earful from her on that subject later.

The thing that really got to me, though, was that this wasn't the first time I'd needed her to do this for me. I was supposed to be the eldest of the Wheelers. The protector. The one who had his shit together.

But Dana was happily married to a perfectly lovely—if somewhat boring—accountant for a Fortune 500 company. Last Christmas, she'd gone into labor during dinner and delivered a perfect, healthy baby boy. That was the thickest the drama ever got in Dana's life—and then there I was, foisting my playboy problems on her and making her clean up my messes.

I just hoped she knew how much I envied her for that.

I was just polishing off the closing line of my text when I sensed two moving bodies headed straight for me. I moved just in time to avoid a head-on collision—though I wasn't quite fast enough to avoid getting carnival beer splashed onto my boots.

"Oh—fuck. I am *so* sorry. Here, let me…" The beer-splasher dropped to his knees immediately, whipping out a hankie from his pocket that told me immediately he was a local. He quickly set about dabbing the beer off my boots— but when his forest-green eyes glanced up at me, they blinked with surprise. "Royce? Cam didn't mention you'd be out tonight."

A little smile played on my lips as I looked down at Patrick Murray again. "That was rude of him. Considering his opinions on the two of us talking, he should have at least warned you."

"We'll consider it a pleasant surprise, then."

It took me longer than I liked to admit to realize that Patrick's blonde friend was even present. He eyed me with delight, then nudged Patrick with his elbow. "Who's your friend?"

"Right, yeah. This is Royce Wheeler, Tom. Cam's older brother, fresh from the Big Apple. Royce, this is Thomas O'Leery. He's—"

"Leaving, actually," Thomas said with a wink. He gave a little wave to a smirking alpha just behind us and passed me his beer. "It sounds like you two have some catching up to do. I'm sure you'll let me know if you need mama's special fix for grass stains on denim in the morning."

"Tom—hey, no, wait!" Patrick called after his friend as Thomas disappeared into the crowd on the alpha's arm.

"You wanna run after him?" I offered. I liked Patrick—looking at him, mostly—but I also liked the way his ears went pink at a moment's notice. Like they were right now. "If you hurry, you can probably catch him."

"Nah," Patrick said, waving the suggestion away. "Actually, we were just looking for you—or for Cam, really, but it looks like you might be Cam for the night."

"I am," I confirmed. "What's up?"

Patrick cringed. "Might be better if I show you. Wanna head back to the beer tent real quick?"

I grunted in dismay. "Nicky?"

Patrick gave a strained laugh. "Yeah … I hate to be the one to tell you this, but you probably shouldn't have left him alone there."

"Fuck," I swore. "All right, let's boogie—before that little shit burns the entire beer garden down around him."

"It's not a bad night for a barbecue," Patrick joked, slipping his hand into mine. "So we don't get separated. Crowd's crazy tonight."

I didn't know how to tell him that he didn't need to give me an excuse to touch him. Cam might have put us on notice, but that didn't mean I was opposed to a little innocent hand-holding.

In fact, it was kind of nice—even though, knowing what I knew of Nicky, whatever we found when we got back to the beer tent would be anything but.

Chapter 4

Patrick

Royce stood there at the beer tent, pinching the bridge of his nose between his index finger and his thumb.

"Okay," he said, shoulders heaving like he was bearing the full weight of Nicky's asinine behavior across his back. "Explain this to me again. Walk me through it. Make me understand how you thought this was a good idea."

Nicky eyed the fuzzy pink handcuff locked around his wrist. The other end left him locked around one of the poles holding the beer tent up.

"In my defense," he said, "He was *very* cute—and I never thought it was a *good* idea."

"Then why the hell did you let that asshole cuff you?"

Nicky shrugged. "Seemed like fun at the time."

"And now?"

Nicky eyed the pink fluff clasped tight around his wrist again. "Admittedly, less fun. Help me outta these things?"

Royce's shoulders heaved once more, but he only grumbled gently under his breath as he went to Nicky's aid. In all fairness, knowing Nicky, it could have been worse. When Patrick and I had gotten our beers, we'd found him cuffed like that—which had turned Big Hops' beer tent into more of a self-service, pay-what-you-like establishment than the Wheeler boys would have preferred.

I didn't know how Royce expected to get Nicky out of the cuffs without a key—but Royce obviously had a plan. I watched with interest as he forced his fingers between Nicky's slender wrist and the pink fur of the cuff. He gave a low grunt and a quick, sharp yank, and the cuff yielded to Royce's brute force and popped open with ease.

"Should've left you here all night." Royce dropped the cuff and let it slide to the ground. "Would've served you right, you know."

"What? So some big, strong alpha could come along and take advantage of little ol' me? Goodness, what a *terrible* fate." Nicky fanned himself as he stationed himself back at the till.

"Omegas," Royce scoffed. He seemed to catch himself as he remembered I was standing right there, though. "Christ, sorry. Present company excluded, of course."

I only shrugged and laughed. "Some of us are like that. Just wait until you get a few more drinks in me. I'll be grinding up against you like an exotic dancer against a stripper pole on rent day."

Then it was my turn to catch myself. "Uh. Sorry. Beer brain."

"You had one too many already tonight?" A teasing smile played on Royce's lips.

"Nah—just enough that my mouth's running faster than my brain can stop it, I think." I glanced over to Nicky, who was in the process of letting a customer pay for his beer by slipping his money into the waistband of Nicky's jeans. "I'm sober enough that I could give you a hand here, if you wanted. The diner serves beer, so I'm licensed and everything."

Royce raised an eyebrow. "Don't want me hanging around Nicky alone, huh?"

"Do *you* want to hang around Nicky alone?"

He laughed. "Good point. Congratulations, Pat—consider yourself hired."

I was glad when Royce turned and waved me behind the card table counter—and not just because it meant I could stare at his ass as I followed him, either. It wasn't until he wasn't looking at me anymore that I realized my hands were absolutely shaking.

I couldn't *believe* what I'd just said to him—or the way I'd said it, for that matter. Normally I was so quiet and reserved. Especially around alphas like Royce. But one lingering gaze from those intense amber eyes and he had me falling over myself, flirting and preening almost much as Nicky was.

It felt nice, admittedly. I'd always imagined what it might be like to be that sensual and confident around an alpha I liked the look of. But it also meant that I'd need to watch myself around Royce. Cam had warned me long ago that Royce was a bit of a playboy, and I wasn't exactly looking for a quick, meaningless fling.

I steadied my hands as I grabbed a cup from the stack and started pouring beers, only casting the occasional glance—or four—in Royce's direction. He was nice to look at, sure, but I knew before long he'd be back in the big city, cavorting around with the glamorous omegas who lived there, and I'd be here in Carter's Crossing, still trying to make up my mind about what I wanted to do with my life.

We worked side by side for the rest of the night, taking orders and filling them like a well-oiled machine. Every time his fingertips brushed against mine as he handed me a cup, I felt a flush of heat rise up in my cheeks, then flood through the rest of my body—but apart from those few fleeting moments, we both managed to behave ourselves.

It was so easy to get lost in our mechanical tango that by the time the crowd thinned, we realized that Nicky had slipped away without us even noticing.

"Ungrateful little horndog," Royce scoffed. "You mind helping me pack up? I'm not against giving you Nicky's cut of the pay for tonight. He obviously doesn't think he needs it."

"I'd be happy to," I told him.

I didn't tell him why: the longer I helped Royce, the longer I could spend time around him. I'd never considered myself clingy before, but basking in the sheer aura of Royce's charisma and masculinity felt too delicious to pass up.

He was practically magnetic, with the way he seemed to control any space he entered. I saw more than one interested omega give me an envious glance as their alpha partners paid their tabs that night. They must have thought that Royce and I were together somehow.

If only they knew how wrong they were.

"You need a ride home?" Royce offered, once the last of the empty kegs was packed away. "I'm stone cold sober—I can drop you off, if you like."

"You don't have to go out of your way like that," I assured him. "I'll take a ride back to the brewery with you, though. If you unload this truck by yourself, you'll be there all night."

"Deal," Royce said, sticking out a hand for me to shake. "I'll take you back to your place after. It'll be late either way, and I hear these mountain roads get a little dangerous at night."

I hesitated before putting my hand in his. Any mention of danger on the mountain roads left me thinking of my alpha dad and Devil's Bend. It wasn't a nice thing to be reminded of, anytime anyone told me to drive safe or complained about the mountain weather, but ultimately I'd learned how to push it out of my mind.

There was no point in ruining a perfectly good night thinking about the sadness of the past. Not when I'd be spending the rest of it at the side of an alpha like Royce, at any rate.

He had to help me up into the passenger seat of the brewery truck—or at least, he was convinced that he had to, and I let him believe it. Despite all Cam's talk of Royce's playboy nature, he was quite the gentleman. It still impressed me that he'd set Nicky free from whatever weird scenario he'd gotten himself into with the handcuffs. Despite Royce's grumblings after, I was pretty sure I would have left Nicky there to sort out his own problems.

"How did you know how to do that?" I asked suddenly, as Royce guided the truck down the mountain road. "With Nicky's handcuff situation, I mean. You popped them open like it was nothing."

Royce kept his eyes on the road but let a slight, wicked smile appear on his lips. "As much as I wish I could say it was brute force—it wasn't. Whoever handcuffed Nicky to that pole wasn't serious about it. If he was, he would've gotten stronger handcuffs. The cheap gag gift ones always break like that."

"Do you know a lot about handcuffs?" I found myself asking.

Royce let out a bark of a laugh. "You want the answer to that question, you'll have to come back to my place and find out for yourself."

Maybe I'd like that, I thought—but at least I didn't say *that* out loud. I'd done enough word vomit that night to tide me over for a full lifetime—and Cam certainly wouldn't appreciate me taking his brother up on the offer.

If it even was an offer, I reminded myself. He'd probably been kidding. Royce was a notorious flirt. He'd lived up to Cam's stories about him in that regard, at least.

"So what was it like growing up with Cam?" I asked, veering the topic to safer territory. "Was he such an unforgivable hipster even as a kid, or did that come later?"

"College," Royce verified. "As soon as he got into Neutral Milk Hotel and got his first undercut, it was all over for Cam."

We talked and joked about Royce's family the rest of the way back to the brewery. Royce was a great storyteller—he had this way of making every yarn he spun come to life with nothing more than the sound of his voice.

But as we finished unloading the truck, the conversation turned back to the romantic again—and this time, Royce couldn't seem to help himself. "So you and Cam," he said. "What ended it?"

"Nothing serious." I helped him settle the final empty keg into place for the night. "I guess, even though he's older than me, he always seemed pretty young at heart. Your brother is …a little wild for my tastes, honestly. I always felt like I was getting whiplash trying to keep up with him."

"Funny." Royce's fingertips lingered on the keg after he'd finished moving it, just fractions of an inch away from my own. "You don't seem like the kind of guy who'd have a hard time keeping up with anyone."

"Maybe not. But when they're so much older than me…"

"So you like older men."

"Sometimes," I said softly. "When they can behave themselves, I do."

"And what if they're not good at behaving themselves?"

Royce's fingertips brushed against my own. I turned to him and he drew closer, invading my space. He was tall, and broad, and built as sturdily as the mountains that Carter's Crossing was perched in. I found my breath catching in my throat just being this close to him.

Close enough to pick up his scent, breathe in his cologne.

He took my jaw in the palm of his hand and dipped his head. Royce stopped just before his mouth crushed against mine, making me lean forward if I wanted to claim what he was offering.

A kiss. Just one little kiss—how bad could it be?

I took him up on it, leaning into him and letting him kiss me. He tasted like mint gum and bad decisions. Something stirred in me that I was having a hard time denying.

I pulled away, ending the kiss almost as quickly as it had started. I did it because I had to—because if I'd kept on kissing him, it wouldn't have ended there.

Royce set a fire in me that was hard to put out. But I had to—I didn't have a choice.

"We … we can't do this," I said softly as he ran his thumb over my cheekbone, looking down at me with concern. "With your brother being my ex and all … it just wouldn't be right."

"Sorry," Royce apologized immediately. "The flirting—I misread some signals, obviously."

"It's my own fault," I said with a nervous laugh. "You weren't misreading them—I just shouldn't have been sending them. A man like you … you can make a guy like me forget myself."

"Still." Royce backed away. He didn't need to be told twice. "You ready for that ride home?"

"It's not far." I waved his offer away with my hand. "I'll just walk. Won't take long."

"Let me at least walk you, then." Royce held up his hands innocently. "I'll behave myself from here on out—promise."

"Always the gentleman, aren't you?"

"I do what I can," he said with a soft smile.

Royce kept his word the whole way back to my place. At the door, he didn't linger—he only stayed for long enough to make sure I got in all right.

I missed his presence as soon as he was gone. Coupled with the loud, sporadic creaking of Tom's bed frame, and the periodic thumping of it against the wall we shared between our rooms, the feeling only got worse.

Two simultaneous, passionate moans told me that Tom had obviously found himself a friend for the night—and there I was again. In my own bed. Alone.

And it was my own damn fault, too. If I were honest with myself, it wasn't the fact that Royce was Cam's brother that had stopped me from letting that kiss take its course. It was the fact that I knew one night with Royce would only ever *be* one night.

Tom might have been good at taking random hookups as they presented themselves, but I didn't have that in me. I wanted something deeper—something richer—something *more*.

But no matter how much I might have wanted it with Royce, I knew better. Big city playboy comes to small town to deflower hopeless-romantic country boy—that tale was older than either of us. I wasn't looking for a quick story to trade with Tom over beers tomorrow night. I wanted a happily ever after.

And as far as things with Royce went, I'd need to start looking elsewhere.

Chapter 5

Royce

"Would you look at that? She's ready, boys!" Cam stepped back with pride, holding a beer stein beneath the tap of his latest lager as a dark, foamy amber beer gushed out of it. "Drinks for everyone today—on the house!"

"After that last batch he tried foisting off onto us, I think I'll pass," I heard Nicky mutter under his breath.

Nicky's curiosity must have gotten the better of him in the end, though. He raised his glass high with the rest of us as we took our first tentative sips of Cam's new lager—the one that, if successful, could wind up saving the brewery once and for all.

The taste of citrus, cloves, and the brewery's infamous hops poured over my tongue. Unlike the last batch, this was clean, crisp and pleasantly sweet.

"This is … surprisingly good." I was the first to speak—everyone else seemed to still be drinking.

"Surprisingly?" Cam wiped some foam from his lip and cackled with delight. "This is incredible, you asshole."

I clapped Cam on the back and laughed along with him. "Congrats, man. I think she's a keeper."

It had been several weeks since my ill-fated kiss with Patrick—not that I'd bothered telling Cam about it. If Patrick had mentioned it to him, Cam had been too busy focusing on his brew recipe to chide me for it.

As for Patrick himself, I'd only seen him in passing since the kiss. It seemed like he was a little more cautious around me in the wake of our moment of weakness—which was probably a good thing.

He was a damn good kisser, that Patrick Murray. If he hadn't stopped me that night, I would have had him in my bed in a hot minute, just to see what those lips could do when they moved a little further south.

In hindsight, though, it had been the right call. I was still Cam's guest here, after all. At the very least, Patrick had saved us a particularly awkward walk of shame the next morning.

"I guess we'll need a name. I don't suppose you keep any ideas on tap around here," I commented, taking another sip.

"Not even enough of 'em to fill a shot glass," Cam admitted. "But that's what you're here for, right?"

"How about *Spank Me, Daddy?*" Nicky mused with a coy grin.

"No." Cam and I shut him down in unison.

"Nothing dirty," I added. "It's got too clean of a finish—and we want this to be something we can export wide. I want to see this thing in supermarkets, not just on tap at Big Mike's."

"How about Spank Me, Daddy, *Please*?" Cam joked.

We roared with laughter before sitting down with his crew and spitballing for a little while. It was one of the worst parts about marketing, honestly. Once you had a good product, it needed a name that was both memorable and *right*. And even then, we'd need the right art for the label, a distribution plan, some formal tastings...

Cam might have polished off the legwork on his end of things, but I had my work cut out for me moving forward. I was glad I still had a month and a half of vacation time left to orchestrate all of the rest.

Unless I didn't go back to New York at all, I guessed … but I was still deciding on that. I probably would be until the last possible second, really.

On the one hand, I loved the big city life. On the other, I didn't exactly want to be in the same zip code as yet another of my cheating exes again—or my scoundrel of a boss.

It was strange, being back here in Carter's Crossing. The streets all had the same names, and I could still pick out plenty of familiar faces in any crowd, but it felt different, too. The town hadn't changed all that much—it rarely did—which meant I was the one who must have come back different.

Big-city life had spoiled me, I realized. Made me think I was something bigger, more important, more glamorous than I really was. But despite it all, Carter's Crossing still felt like home to me. Being back here after such a prolonged absence made me feel like I was finally getting back to my roots.

"This calls for pie," Cam announced, once his crew had finally meandered home for the day. "Want me to get Patrick to bring you a piece too?"

I shook my head. "I'll keep my six-pack as it is, thanks."

"Whatever you say, man. More for me."

As I watched Cam open up his texts with Patrick on his phone, a little wave of guilt washed over me. It was already a bit awkward when Patrick showed up with a lunch delivery for Cam—and that was when there were other people around. I couldn't imagine how he might feel to be stuck in a room with just me and my brother, his pie-crazed ex.

"Speaking of Patrick … there's something I ought to come clean about."

Cam groaned without looking up from his phone. "You fucked him, didn't you?"

"No," I reassured him. "Nothing like that. I did make a move on him, however—one he turned down, might I add. There *may* have been a kiss involved. Nothing more than that, though. Promise."

Cam flashed a wicked grin at me. "He's a good kisser, isn't he?"

I felt my jaw tense as I was reminded that Cam probably knew a lot more than that about Patrick's more carnal talents—but still, there was no denying it.

"He is. I can see why you're territorial about him. Hoping you two will get back together, huh?"

"Ha. Hardly. Patrick's a sweetheart, but it was never going to work out between us. That ship has *sailed.*"

I raised an eyebrow. "Then why so possessive?"

Cam sighed. "Man, I just don't want him to get hurt. We're friends, you know? If you go lovin' and leavin' that poor boy, he'll get his heart broken—and then who am I gonna bully into bringing me pie on demand?"

Cam pursed his lips in intense concentration. "Cherry or pumpkin … mm. Or blueberry?"

"Pumpkin," I said. "It'll pair well with the lager. What makes you think I'll break his heart, though?"

Cam laughed. "Please, Roy. You only have two types of relationships under your belt: the kind that end with your omega's mouth around someone else's dick, and the kind that end when the sun comes up. Hit-it-and-quit-it is your specialty."

"And he doesn't seem like the cheating type." I ran my thumb along my jawline. "So say that I wanted to change up my game a little. Would you still be against it?"

"Honestly?" Cam looked up from his phone, leveling with me. "If you're so hung up over him, ask him out on a real date and see what happens.

"He's not the casual hook-up type—so if you're planning on leading him on just to get him into bed with you, I'll superglue your ball sac to your asshole while you're asleep and let you suffer the consequences."

"I'm not that kind of guy, Cam. You know me better than *that,* I hope."

"Good. Because he'll be here with the pumpkin pie in fifteen minutes." Cam grinned. "And the cherry. Couldn't decide."

When Patrick swung in with the pie, as expected, he kept his distance. Exactly as I'd feared—I'd come on way too strong that night he'd helped me out with the beer garden. Flirtatious, vivacious Patrick was gone—for now. It didn't make me like him any less.

I was beginning to think that Cam was right. I *did* have a pattern, though it hadn't done me any good so far. Patrick was definitely the kind of guy I would have fallen into bed with if I'd met him at some bar in New York—and if I'd met him in New York, I probably would have fucked it up royally, like I always seemed to do.

The nice thing about self-realization was that there was always a chance to change things up a bit. When a marketing campaign wasn't giving us what we wanted out of it, we pulled the campaign and started over again. When Cam's beer tasted like old gym socks and soggy grass, he'd changed the recipe.

As Patrick peeled away from Cam and shot me another tentative glance on his way to the door, I called out to him and followed him outside. Whoever said a tiger couldn't change his stripes was a liar. If nothing else, when it came to Patrick, I was at least willing to try.

"You don't have to avoid me, you know," I joked, closing the door behind me.

Patrick rubbed the back of his neck and laughed. "Yeah, I guess that's probably what it looks like I've been doing, huh?"

"Isn't it?"

He shrugged. "I just figured you wouldn't want a lot to do with me after …y'know."

I crossed my arms over my chest, suddenly amused. "And why wouldn't I?"

Patrick raised an eyebrow. "Well, look at you, for one." He gestured up and down my body. "You could have your pick of any omega in town, Royce. You don't have any reason to go sniffing around the one who was dumb enough to turn you down."

"First off, I don't think you're dumb." I hated hearing people put themselves down like that—especially people who were as charming as Patrick was. He just hadn't realized it yet. "Second off—who says I'm sniffing around? Not all alphas are feral dogs, you know."

He laughed. "Just like not all omegas are bitches in heat. Yeah, makes sense. Still—seems like, the way we left things, it was best if I gave you some space. After that kiss … there's not a lot left to say between us … is there?"

Maybe I was wrong, but I detected some level of hopefulness in his voice. Now that Patrick was watching himself a little more carefully around me, I was quickly beginning to realize how close to his chest he could play things when he wanted. I was usually pretty good at reading people—had to be, in my industry—and even I was having a hard time figuring him out now.

"You tell me," I finally said. "I was just thinking how nice it would be to take you out for dinner sometime. Italian, maybe? There's a good place up on Fifth and Main if I remember right, and you're probably just about as sick of diner food as I am of beer."

Patrick opened his mouth like he was ready to answer immediately, then stopped himself before he could get the words out. "I … I don't know. Cam…"

"Cam's fine with it. Really. You're welcome to clear it with him if you want."

Patrick bit his lower lip in a way that made my inner alpha lick his horny lips—but eventually, he nodded and gave me a soft smile. "Pasta and wine might be a nice change of pace, actually. And it'd be good to get to know you better—I really did have fun that night."

"Good. Give me your number, then. How's Saturday work for you? Pick you up at, say, eight?"

"Make it seven, and it's a deal." His grin turned sly as I produced my phone for him to key his number into. "My glass slippers turn back into Converse All-Stars at midnight, I'm afraid."

"Don't you worry, Cinderella. I'll be sure to have you home before your fairy godmother has to give you a talking to."

"Thomas isn't … quite that kind of fairy godmother. More likely than not, he'll just want to grill me for all the dirty details."

"Dirty, huh?" I smiled as he tapped his number into my phone, then passed it back to me. "Is that how you like your fairy tales, Patrick Murray?"

"I might." My heart ba-dumed and my cock twitched as the tip of Patrick's tongue slid over his lower lip. "As long as there's a happy ending."

"I'll see what I can do," I said, not even trying to keep the innuendo from my voice.

Patrick grinned again before his smile turned almost bashful. "It's a date, then."

I laughed as I heard the tiniest upward inflection on the end of that statement. Like he was asking me a question—like despite the promise of a fancy sit-down dinner, good pasta and Italian wine, he still wasn't sure.

"Yes," I confirmed. "It's a date."

Chapter 6

Patrick

Saturdays were the one day of the week that I always found time to draw. The high school kids were free to man the diner over the weekend, and eager for the hours, so I didn't have any shifts to pick up. If I went over the books on Sundays, I could clear all of Saturday to work on my various art projects to my heart's content.

If it was a good day, I'd finish three or four sketches. If I was working on something a little more complex, I might only finish one or two. The important thing was that I didn't usually spend a lot of time perfecting each one. By the end of the week, I was so absolutely bursting with creative energy that I couldn't really control myself.

I'd read some anecdote about college students making clay pots somewhere that supported this compulsion. Apparently, when you told half of your art school students to spend the entire semester making one clay pot upon which their final grade would rest, while the other half were told they'd be judged on quantity, the students churning out the most work also ended up creating the best work by the end of the semester.

That was where I was with art—the churning phase. If I had it my way, I'd spend all week churning—but as it was, Saturdays would have to do.

On that particular Saturday, though, I was struggling. I'd started a piece with a single figure, half in shadow, walking down a long, sharply curved road. But at some point in the piece, a second figure had shown up. It had thrown off my shading entirely, and every time I went back to fix one element, I managed to screw up three more things.

By the time the alarm on my phone buzzed, alerting me that I had a pathetic half an hour to get ready for my big date with Royce, I was covered in charcoal and ready to tear my hair out over the damn sketch. I was still fuming over it when I got out of the shower and gave my hair a quick blow dry. Hell, I was still fuming about it as I pulled on my dress shoes and headed out the door to Royce's car.

In a way, I guessed I was lucky that I'd been so caught up in my work while I was getting ready. Because as soon as I saw Royce standing there, leaning up against the passenger-side door of his sleek black car, dressed in a muscle-hugging, charcoal button-down, my heart skipped a beat.

I was *nervous* for this date with Royce. I'd been too frustrated earlier to realize it, but now that I was confronted with the insanely handsome alpha waiting to whisk me away for pasta and wine for the evening, I was flustered. Butterflies in my stomach? Check. Pulse racing? Double check.

By the time he opened his arms to hug me, I was half-hard and in danger of sweating through my own dress shirt. But I'd forgotten how good Royce was at smoothing things over just by being himself. It was hard to feel too nervous around him—he gave off that quintessential alpha vibe that so few alphas ever managed to master. In control, but not overly domineering. Relaxed, but not so chill that I felt like I didn't matter.

"It's good to see you," he said, pressing a kiss to my cheek.

"Likewise," I managed to choke out with a smile.

Royce opened the door for me and took my hand to help me in. The care that he took as he did it made me feel oddly … important. I knew he was just being a gentleman, but I couldn't recall anyone else ever treating me like that before.

Dinner started off a little more formal than I'd expected, which I was surprised to find I didn't mind. Royce was more reserved than he'd been when we'd first met—maybe because I wasn't falling over myself to announce that I was a fertile omega in desperate need of breeding anymore. As we ordered our pasta, a couple of times I was sure I caught him staring at me, like he was studying some obscure piece of art in a museum.

I was giving him nothing to work with, I realized—and still, he was investing his time in trying to figure me out. "Sorry," I finally said. "I'm … bad at this."

"Bad at what? Eating spaghetti?" He eyed the way I was endlessly twisting my pasta on the end of my fork and leaned over, chuckling slightly. "Here—the secret is, you've gotta really ground your fork. Show it you mean business."

He took my hand and showed me how to press down on the plate with just a little more force. The result was a perfectly twirled mouthful of pasta. I grinned at him as I patted my lips clean with my napkin, an explosion of tomato sauce and herbs on my tongue.

"Where'd you learn that? Let me guess … Milan?"

Royce narrowed his eyes at me. "What do you know about Milan?"

"Cam may have told me … a thing or two."

Royce groaned. "He told you the Speedo story, didn't he."

My eyes widened. "He did *not*—I was thinking about the one with the Italian model, who couldn't seem to remember which one of you he was dating. But now that you mention it, I would love to hear *any* story involving you, Milan, and a Speedo."

Royce cringed, then leaned back and took a deep breath. "Well … see, Cam thought it would be funny to tell me that the omegas there preferred a man with shaved legs."

I gasped, pressing my fingertips to my lips to avoid laughing at him outright. "Holy shit, he didn't."

"Being the only one of us who spoke Italian at the time, Cam did most of the wheeling and dealing when we did our study abroad there," Royce explained. "Thus, the model. Cam brought him home the night before—I just happened to be the only one around the next morning."

"Do you always end up with Cam's sloppy seconds?" I teased.

"I resent that," Royce said with a laugh. "Just for that, I won't tell you how the Speedo story ends."

"No!" I dove across the table, taking his hand in mine with earnest. *"Please* tell me the rest of the Speedo story."

"Right," Roy said with a nod, setting the scene. "Picture a beautiful, white-sand beach, ocean waves rolling in … and now picture me, wearing only the tiniest little yellow thong that Europe could provide, not a single hair on me past my eyebrows, and oiled up so slick I could have slipped through a keyhole if I'd had the notion to."

I raised my eyebrows. "Sounds majestic."

And it did—Royce in a Speedo was probably a sight to behold, hair or no hair.

"I'm sure it was," Royce agreed. "Until we got into a beach volleyball match with the locals, anyway. I dove for the ball, and *bam!* Covered in sand from head to toe. I got sand in places I didn't even realize existed—and fuck, it itched for the rest of the day, too."

We both laughed too hard and finished up our glasses of wine over that mental image. And just like that, the formalness of the date had dissolved. When the waiter came to pour a second glass, Royce turned him down, but gave me a nod.

"I've got to drive—but you should have another if you want."

I smiled at him as the waiter poured me a second glass. "Did you ever go back to Milan?"

"Once," Royce admitted. "With my last boyfriend. Now ex, of course. I took him there for our one-year back in June. It was…"

A brief scowl crossed Royce's face. "It was fine. My boss spent most of the trip putting me on bullshit tasks that probably could have waited until I got back, so we didn't get to spend much time together, but otherwise it was an okay trip."

"June?" I blinked in surprise. "You guys must not have broken up long ago, then."

"It doesn't matter now." Royce turned back to his gnocchi and shook his head. "Sorry for ranting. How's the pasta?"

The conversation turned back to the mundane quickly, and I had half a notion why. If Royce was fresh out of a relationship, it was no wonder that talking about his ex had turned him off. It made me a little worried that he wasn't entirely over this mysterious ex—especially since he didn't really seem engaged again until the drive home.

"Sorry—you know this turn up ahead?" I said anxiously, pointing it out for him.

"Devil's Bend," Royce said with a nod. "Don't worry—I always honk."

"Thanks. My dads…"

Royce glanced over at me for a moment, then slowed his speed a little and tapped his horn. Relieved, I found myself breathing a little easier once we'd made it safely around the turn.

"You were saying?" he asked, with what I hoped was interest.

"My dads took the turn without thinking one night. A semi truck came blasting around from the other direction a little too fast and hydroplaned. Bumped our car with the back end of his trailer and sent it crashing down the mountain. My … my alpha dad didn't make it."

I stared at my lap, suddenly embarrassed that I'd even brought it up. "I was only three at the time. Probably for the best that I wasn't old enough to remember it."

Royce placed his hand on my knee comfortingly as he pulled up to my driveway. "It's good that you can talk about it, Patrick. I'm a little touched that you felt comfortable sharing it with me."

"I'm embarrassed that I made you listen to it," I blurted out before I could stop myself. "I … I don't want you to think I've got some sob story for every occasion or something. I don't dwell on it. Just, that turn makes me a little nervous, is all. My omega dad is the same way."

"I don't think it's a sob story," Royce said softly, giving my knee a little squeeze. "Let me walk you to your front door?"

I nodded, and Royce jogged around to the passenger side of the car so he could open my door for me. As he helped me out of the car, I couldn't help but smile.

"You know, you're not making me feel any better by doting on me like this," I told him with a little laugh.

"Please. You deserve to be doted on." He raised an eyebrow suddenly. "Unless you'd prefer me to be a jackass? I've lived in New York for long enough now, I could probably pull off the jackass thing with ease."

"Yes," I urged him jokingly. "Please, promise to take out the trash for me but never follow through on it."

"Only if you'll make me a sandwich first. I only eat bologna on Wonder Bread, and if you don't cut the crust off, I'll make you re-do the whole thing."

"You must be a real dream of a boyfriend, Royce," I joked—then blushed as I realized I might have taken the joke too far.

Royce only laughed, though. "Just wait until you see me in a Speedo, sweetheart. I'll shave so thoroughly, you'll be finding my body hair in your bathroom for the next three years. At least."

"Can't wait," I told him as we came up to my front door. He lingered, and I found myself lingering along with him. Even though the date was over, I couldn't help but want more. "Thank you for tonight. I honestly had a really good time."

"We'll have to do it again sometime, then," Royce agreed. I saw him glance at my lips, then briefly run his tongue across his own. "Can I kiss you, Patrick? Because—fuck, I'd really like to kiss you right now."

Just like that, my breath grew short again, and my heart pounded harder than ever. Royce Wheeler was a force to be reckoned with. He was sexy as hell when he was claiming kisses with reckless, domineering abandon—and he was sexy as hell when he was asking for them, like some kind of old-fashioned gentleman who had to wait until he'd put a ring on my finger before he could ask to come inside.

"Please," I gasped, before I had a chance to second-guess myself.

And then there we were again, locking lips and wrapped in each other's arms. The kiss wasn't quite as steamy as our first, but that wouldn't have felt right. This one was more reserved—it was the kind of kiss that told me that Royce *could* behave himself. When he wanted to. With someone he wanted to behave for.

"Tell me I can take you out again," he commanded—although there was a softness in his eyes as he said it that made me feel like I could still say no if I wanted to.

When it came to Royce, though, no was the last thing on my mind. "If you're okay with taking things slow," I told him. "I don't rush into things—even for men with lips like yours."

"Slow," Royce said with a gentle nod. "I can do slow." His eyes raked up and down my body and I shivered. "I won't always like it, mind you … but I can manage it."

Even with just a look, Royce could get me hard in an instant. My body was drawn to him in a way that didn't really appreciate *slow* either—but my body could just deal with it.

But as he walked away, casting a final glance over his shoulder at me, it wasn't my body that I was worried about—when it came to Royce, it was my heart that was in danger of being broken.

The thing with his ex worried me more than I liked to admit. The date had definitely hit a snag when the subject came up, and he'd been quick to shift gears away from it, too. It made me wonder … was he really over the guy? Or was he still carrying a torch for him?

They were questions that were just as frustrating as the direction my sketch of the day was taking. I sat up all night, mulling them over while I tried to get the proportions on the figures right—and come morning, neither problem had sorted itself out.

Chapter 7

Royce

Sneaking back into Camden's place after my date with Patrick reminded me of the way I used to tiptoe up the stairs at our dads' place after a long night of sowing my wild oats back in high school. It reminded me of it because despite my age, not a lot had changed since then. I was still fucking bad at it—and just like in high school, I still managed to get caught.

"Roy?" Cam came out of his office and flipped the kitchen light on just as I was trying to oh-so-quietly close the front door. He glanced down at his watch and back up in surprise. "Wow—you're back earlier than I thought."

"Waiting up for me, huh?"

Cam laughed. "Roy, it's not even midnight yet. I was about to crack open a lager and brainstorm some more name ideas. Come on—I'll grab you one too, and you can tell me about your wild night."

I shrugged. "Not much to tell, man. I don't think your ex likes me much."

Cam narrowed his eyes as he opened the fridge "Why? Did he say so?"

"Said he wanted to take things slow." I accepted one of the bottled lagers gratefully and twisted the cap off with the heel of my hand. "Pretty sure that's omega code for *I'm just not that into you.*"

"Patrick? No way." Cam reached out to take my bottle cap, and I dropped it in his hand. "Patrick doesn't do the whole *no means yes* thing—and believe me, he's *very* vocal about what he does and doesn't want."

I raised an eyebrow with interest. "Sound like there's a story there."

Cam groaned. "Didn't I tell you how he broke up with me?" He cleared his throat and raised his voice half an octave as he launched into one of his notoriously bad impressions. "*Camden, I really appreciate you as a friend, but I just don't think this will ever be anything more than that. As much as I would love to spread my gorgeous cheeks for you and give you more babies than you can handle, I just—oof!*"

Cam doubled over as I elbowed him gently in the gut. "Let me guess," I said with a laugh. "You got too drunk one night, tried to convince him to let you go at him without a condom on, and he dumped your ass so hard you got road rash."

"No, actually. I feel deeply hurt and slandered that you'd even suggest such a thing" Cam cleared his throat and straightened a little. "If you *must* know, Patrick and I only dated for a couple of months and never got past first base. He's careful like that, man. I'm telling you, he doesn't do casual—and if he doesn't like you, you'll know it."

I took a long swig of my beer, mulling this new bit of information over. "Well, that makes me feel a hell of a lot better about chasing your ex, at least. He asked me tonight if I always got your sloppy seconds—can you believe that."

Cam nearly spat out his beer. "You guys talked about Mario? Oh, *god.* You're really flubbing this one, Roy."

I rolled my eyes. "You're telling me. I brought up the fucking Speedo story too."

"On second thought, maybe he's *not* into you. Although, if he agreed to a second date after hearing about how you shaved off all your body hair…"

I nodded in agreement. "We're past the point of no return on that one, yeah. He *did* say he wanted to see me again, though."

Cam patted me on the shoulder. "Good for you, man. You're finally learning how to date like an actual adult. Took you long enough."

"Like you have room to talk. Didn't your last boyfriend threaten to torch the brewery when you two broke up?"

Cam waved the criticism away with a laugh. "More than just threatened. We had the police out here and everything. It was a riot, let me tell you."

"Man," I sighed, settling down onto a bar stool at the kitchen island. "Dana really got all the functional relationship genes in the family, huh?" We clinked our beer bottles together in solidarity. "At least the dads have one kid they can be proud of."

"You know … there *is* something you should know about Patrick. Before you take things any further, I mean. Normally, I wouldn't mention it, but—well, you're you, and like I said, Patrick is a friend."

"I'm me?" I sipped at my beer, unsure of whether to be offended or amused.

"You're a Wheeler alpha." Cam gave an eye roll. "And I'm pretty sure Patrick is a virgin. He's dated here and there, but as far as I know … nothing's really stuck, if you catch my drift."

I turned back to my beer. It was something I'd considered, sure. Sometimes, you could just tell. There was a hesitation to Patrick that made a strong case for sexual inexperience.

But it could have just meant that Patrick was selective. Picky. In a way, I guessed he was—so picky, in fact, that he hadn't chosen *anyone* yet.

On one level, it simplified things. Virgin omegas had every right to be picky. They didn't know how fucking *good* sex could be—or how bad, depending on the alpha. On another level, it only made things between Patrick and I more difficult. If there wasn't a single alpha in Carter's Crossing who'd tickled his fancy, then what the hell would he want with a forty-year-old romantic fuck-up like me?

Sure, I had the looks. I had the abs. I had the big-city money and the luxury car. But in terms of real emotional intimacy, I was just as much of a romantic virgin as Patrick was a physical one.

Maybe that was why I'd ended up with so many omegas who'd cheated on me the first chance they got. Despite my sexual prowess, on the emotional side of things, I couldn't say that I'd ever gone all-in. Going all in with Patrick, though … I'd be lying if I said it didn't make my cock swell a little to think that I might be his first.

I must have been considering that particular dirty thought a little too hard, though. "You dirty dog." Cam narrowed his eyes and shook his head, laughing at me. "It's turning you on, thinking about taking that boy's virginity and showing him all your wicked ways, isn't it?"

"It's not," I lied, pointing at Cam authoritatively. "But you wanna keep teasing me about it, I'll be sure to tell him how *you* lost *your* virginity while we're basking in the afterglow."

"You wouldn't."

"Oh, I would. He'll never be able to look at a pair of red boxers the same way again."

We laughed, drinking and talking for a little while longer, but no matter what topic of conversation Cam brought up, my mind kept wandering back to Patrick. It was a train of thought that—much like my thoughts on the subject of his virginity—must have been broadcast clearly on my face.

"What's eating you, Royce? I've never seen you this pensive without an expense report in front of your face."

I shook my head. "Just my romance woes, Cam. Same as always. This whole Patrick thing is proving to be a tough nut to crack."

"If it's cracking a nut you're after, I'm pretty sure Nicky's always open to new gentlemen callers." Cam laughed at his own joke, but it faded into a more serious look.

"But if this is really the new you, Roy … I've gotta say, I think it's a good change for you. Patrick's the kind of guy who could really make you happy if you're willing to put in the time with him. Ask him about his art next time you two hang out—he'll downplay it like a motherfucker, but he's damn good at it."

"Art, huh?" I appreciated the advice—it'd be good to have something to talk to him about other than the dumbass things Cam and I had done in our twenties, at least. "Thanks for the chat, Cam. See you in the morning?"

"I'd better. We've got a lager to name, remember?"

After we said our goodnights, I hopped in the shower and let the hot water wash away my worries. Patrick was young, sure—and potentially virginal to boot—but I could also tell that there was a lot for me to unpack and discover about him yet. The art thing was only one of many interesting new developments that evening, and I was looking forward to coercing him into showing me his work.

But as I soaped myself up and felt my muscles relax with the steam, I found my thoughts turning away from the emotional and back to the physical again—just like they always did. I hadn't slept with a virgin omega since college, and even then … somehow, with Patrick's tenderness and my experience, I knew that it would be so much better than any fumbling, half-drunk dorm-room hookup.

As I imagined the mechanics of it—bending Patrick over, feeling his heat as I kissed his neck and rimmed my thumb around his tight, virginal hole—my cock got hard enough that I had to take it in my fist. I stroked myself to the thought of him gasping my name, crying out in perfect ecstasy as I pistoned in and out of him.

I imagined him begging—no, *pleading* with me. He'd held out on finding a mate for so long, I wanted him dripping for me. Desperate.

And once he was, I'd fill him with every last drop of cum my balls had to offer.

Then I'd take him again. And again. Until he trembled with longing every time he so much as looked at me, and when his cock got hard, it was because of my name on his lips.

But sex wasn't the name of the game, not yet. Intimacy was what Patrick and I needed if this flirtation was ever going to turn into something more.

I came with a growl, imagining his perfect lips wrapped around my shaft. But for that night, all I could have was my fantasies. In place of the real thing, I was leaving room for something better.

Something more.

Chapter 8

Patrick

"Okay, buttercup," Thomas announced as he kicked in my door. He held a pot of coffee in one hand and an entire bunch of bananas in the other—which struck me as particularly eccentric, even for Tom. "Time to take sustenance and tell me why you're moping around like a toad on frog catchin' day."

"Like a what?" I eyed the bananas and coffee with suspicion. "Tom, you know that coffee and bananas doesn't really count as sustenance, right?"

"Why not. Caffeine—" He raised the pot of coffee a little higher, then lowered it and raised the bananas. "And potassium. Two of the five major food groups. It's a start."

I snickered, straightening and turning around in my desk chair. "What are the other three?"

"Alcohol, semen and daddy's breakfast grits." He dropped the bunch of bananas on my desk and retreated for a moment, coming back in with a coffee mug. "I figured we'd start with the easy ones first and get a little more ambitious from there."

"I'm fine, Tom. Really."

"Not what it looks like."

I moved my arm instinctively to cover the drawing I'd been working on. It was a Thursday, not a Saturday, but ever since my date with Royce and my dad's latest update to his retirement plans, I'd been stealing every chance I could to work a little more on my sketching. It was unlike me to still be working on the same piece nearly a week after I'd started it, but the harder I worked at it, the more it seemed to elude me.

Normally, by now, I would have just scrapped it—written it off and moved on to something new—but there was something about this piece that was really speaking to me. It needed work, sure, but for some reason, I felt like it might actually pay off to put in my time on it—no matter how long it took.

"I've just been … I don't know. Busy, I guess. Dad keeps upping my hours at the diner, and when he's not trying to teach me management techniques, he's trying to set me up with his friends' alpha sons. It's been a messy week."

"So you're spending what little free time you *do* have holed up in your room like this? Jeez, Pat—at least tell me what you're working on."

I shifted my arm over further, blocking the piece as best I could. "Just a sketch. Nothing serious. It's the only way I've got to blow off steam."

"If you really want to blow off steam, you ought to see what that hunky alpha I left you with at the carnival is up to. I bet he'd help you blow off all *sorts* of things." Tom poured me a cup of coffee and shoved it my way across the desk. "Drink. You know, if you locked him down as a boyfriend, your dad would stop trying to set you up."

"He just wants to get in my pants." I rolled my eyes and sniffed at the coffee. I'd taken to distrusting most things he whipped up in the kitchen based on merit alone—he didn't have the attention span for housewifing.

"He's nice," I went on. "Polite, even. But it's pretty clear that he's got the same thing on his mind as every other alpha I've ever gone out with."

"Yikes. That bad, huh?"

I sighed. "His charms got us through the date okay. But I told him about my alpha dad. And I think I set him off about his own ex—who I'm not even sure he's out of love with, to make matters worse."

"Double yikes. What makes you say that?"

Royce's sudden change in attitude when we talked about his ex played over again in my mind. The memory was so fresh still, it was almost like it had only happened a few minutes ago.

"He got a little cagey, I guess. When the ex came up in conversation, I mean. It was like … like I'd dug up something that he was still in the process of burying."

Tom snapped a banana off the bunch and scoffed. "No one likes talking about their exes, Pat. It's miserable conversation. Much like the subject of your alpha dad—no offense. Exes, deaths, and politics have no business on the agenda when it comes to first date talk. Come on, man—you should know better than that."

"Yeah, you'd think." I sipped at the cup of coffee, blanching slightly at its bitterness. Tom had burned it—he almost always did. "But if I'm not making awkward, inappropriate conversation, what the hell will we have left to talk about?"

"Hobbies," Tom suggested. "Interests. How good his cock would look in your mouth."

"Ugh. I'm pretty sure that's the only reason he kept the date going, Tom."

"Can't blame a man for thinkin' about it.Did you tell him about your art?" Tom gestured toward the sketch I was still doing my damnedest to hide from view.

"It didn't occur to me. It's not like I'm some kind of big-time artist, Tom. It's just a little something I do in my free time."

"It's the *only* thing you do in your free time," he corrected me. "You should tell him about it! I'm sure he'd be interested—and then you could start doing him in your free time, too."

"Not going to have any free time for much longer," I grumbled into the coffee cup. Sometimes, coffee got better on the second or third sip. Unfortunately, Tom's coffee tended to start bad and only get worse with further consumption.

I was only drinking it at all because there was caffeine in it and I had a shift in three hours. Maybe Tom was right—it *was* one of the food groups. "Dad finally picked a retirement date, so I can say goodbye to my hobbies *and* my social life."

"Oh, shit," Tom breathed. "When?"

"Three months from now." I breathed in the coffee steam and let it back out on a wistful sigh. "He broke it to me over dinner last night. It seems far away now, but … you know. It's really not, when you think about it."

Tom edged over to sit my desk and thumped his palm down next to my charcoal pencils. "Tell. Him. *Tell him*, Pat. You hate doing business shit! Are you really going to resolve yourself to being unhappy for the rest of your life just because you can't tell your father no?"

"Dad's always been … sensitive," I said, choosing my words carefully. "I don't think he was ever the same after the accident, Tom. I've seen pictures of him before … he used to have the biggest smile on his face all the time.

"Now, it seems like the idea of me taking over the family business is the only thing that really makes me happy. The Lonely Hearts Diner is his legacy— and my alpha dad's, too." I hung my head in defeat. "I don't want to seem ungrateful. I don't think I can turn him down."

"Okay, okay. But just consider—"

Before Tom could maneuver his argument into a different angle, there came three sharp knocks on our front door. Exchanging a glance, we got up to see who it might be. I carried my coffee with me—less because I actually wanted to drink it, and more because it kept my charcoal-stained fingers warm.

"Royce," I said with surprise. "What're you doing here?"

"Hey, Patrick. Tom." He gave Tom a little nod, which impressed me. Considering how briefly they'd met, it was a wonder that he even remembered Tom's name. "I was in your neck of the woods, and wondered if you fancied a walk. It's a nice day out today—weatherman is saying it might be the last one of the season."

I glanced out the door over Royce's shoulder. It was sunny out and gorgeous, with just a hint of fresh-fallen snow powdering the ground. With the fat winter cardinals singing in the evergreens and the promise of Royce's broad, warm body by my side, a walk would be picturesque…

"He'd love to," Tom answered for me. "In fact, he was just mentioning how badly he needed to go stretch his legs—funniest thing!"

Before I could argue, Tom dipped down, grabbed my boots from their place by the door, shoved them against my chest and pushed me out into the cold. By the time I came up with a good reason *not* to go on this little walk with Royce, Tom had already shut the door behind me.

And there wasn't really any point in arguing with *that*.

"Sorry," I said with a laugh as Royce helped steady me. I put the boots on one at a time, using Royce's shoulder to achieve the balancing act it required. "Tom is … a little too enthusiastic sometimes."

"I'm not complaining." Royce gave me a soft smile. "Got you out here with me, didn't it?"

"True. Where are we headed?"

"It's a secret," Royce admitted. "But I *think* you'll like it."

Chapter 9

Royce

For as casual as I'd managed to make this little date seem, I'd put more thought into it than I was willing to let Patrick know. He wasn't like the omegas I'd known in New York, who were, for the most part, generally just concerned with how exclusive of a restaurant I could get us into, or what clubs my company connections could get us on the guest list at. Patrick had so much more depth to him than that.

Where wining and dining had failed to immediately leave Patrick eating out of the palm of my hand, I had a feeling something more down-to-earth might be more to his taste. Camden had mentioned that Patrick was an artist, after all. If there was anything in Carter's Crossing that could truly inspire art, it was what I was about to show him.

"So … how's it going?" When Patrick looked up at me, a little confused, I held his hand up so I could show him I'd noticed all of the charcoal marks on his fingers. "You draw, right?"

He raised his eyebrows, obviously impressed—and a little embarrassed. I could tell from the pink at the tips of his ears. "Yeah," he admitted with a laugh. "A little here and there. I'm surprised you noticed. You're a regular Sherlock Holmes, huh?"

I shook my head, letting out a steamy breath onto his cold fingers, then tucking both of our hands into the pocket of my coat. "Hardly. Cam mentioned it to me the other night, and I've been interested ever since. Why didn't you mention it before?"

Patrick gave a slight shrug. "Didn't seem important enough to work into conversation, I guess. I'm not very good, and it's not like it's anything more than a hobby. I just dabble a little, is all."

"I'd like to see some of your work someday," I admitted honestly. What kind of things did a man like Patrick draw? I wondered if they'd be some kind of clue into all the stuff going on in his head just below the surface—all the things that he was obviously thinking but, for whatever reason, unwilling to actually say out loud. "If you'd do me the honor, I mean."

He waved the suggestion away. "I wouldn't call it much of an honor. I mean, I doubt the cavemen went around dragging their boyfriends back to the cave to show them their half-assed finger paintings."

"Boyfriend, huh?" I caught onto the word and held it as tightly as I held Patrick's hand in mine. I didn't mean to tease him; it was just that he'd been so damn *coy* about everything between us, I felt like I'd earned a little jab here and there. "I don't know, Patrick … this is all moving so fast…"

He smacked my shoulder as I roared with laughter. Our play-fighting sent the birds fleeing from the trees around us as we headed down my favorite nature trail—which was fine by me. The more privacy we had that day, the better, as far as I was concerned.

"You know what I mean," Patrick said, trying to control his grin. "Slip of the tongue, sorry."

"Slip your tongue at me like that again and I might reward you for your efforts." I let go of his hand to put my arm around him and tug him close. "You can't take it back now. Sorry, I won't let you. And for what it's worth, I'd let you drag me back to your cave any day. Finger-painting quality notwithstanding."

"I'd prefer to be the one being dragged, if it's all the same to you." Patrick reached up and tentatively squeezed my bicep. "You've got a better build for kidnapping, I think. With arms like these, you could throw me over your shoulder and carry me off with ease, I don't doubt."

"Maybe so," I agreed, relishing that particular mental image. "But my finger paintings would be far less impressive."

Patrick chuckled. "I don't believe that."

"Nope—not an artistic bone in my body. I just know what I like when I see it." Abruptly, the woods around us ended and opened up into a gorgeous clearing. "That's why I wanted to bring you here. I thought your artist's soul might appreciate it."

Patrick slowly slipped from my side and wandered deeper into the clearing, mouth agape in awe. Even I knew that this place was beautiful—it always was after the first frost.

Just beyond the clearing was a thick, thorny part of the forest that Cam, Dana and I had named the Brambles back when we were kids. Its thickets were glazed over with ice now, creating a dramatic wall of sharp, frosty thorns. The slowing trickle of a waterfall still in the process of freezing over added a little aural ambiance to the scene, as the birds sang overhead and the snow crunched beneath

our feet.

"Royce…this is gorgeous," Patrick breathed. He turned to me, looking at me

in a way I'd never seen him look at anyone before. "This place made you think of

me?"

"I've always liked it here," I said. "I thought maybe you would too. Thought

you might want to draw it sometime. See the way the thorns get darker the further

in you go?" I came up behind him, pointing. "It's always struck me as so severe

and intense—but not any less beautiful because of it."

"For someone with no artistic talent, you sure know how to talk like an

artist," Patrick said with a grin.

"Spent too many years bullshitting my way through the Met gala."

I laughed, and Patrick laughed with me. He was easy to amuse when he

wanted to be. It was one of the many things I liked about him—he didn't take

himself too seriously, and he seemed to know how to appreciate the moment.

Boyfriend or not … I could use someone like him in my life. There was

something so real about Patrick that I'd never found in a guy before.

By the time most omegas got to the city, they were so involved with becoming who they thought they ought to be that they never really figured out who they were. But with Patrick, I could always take him at face value—even as he dipped down, made a snowball, and sent it flying right at my face.

"Oh, I'll make you pay for that," I warned him.

"Why don't you come over here and make me?" he challenged.

The ensuing snowball fight was short-lived—I took that *come over here and make me* part very seriously. After we each lobbed a few snowballs, I ran at Patrick, tackling him to the ground. We rolled in the snow, both of us fighting for dominance for a moment—but of course, being the alpha, I always ended up on top.

As the winner, I was quick to claim my prize. Patrick's lips were cold and soft beneath mine, but I didn't hold back as I warmed him up. This time, when I kissed him, Patrick gave as good as he got. He moved beneath me, just as eager and sultry as he'd been that first night. Maybe even a little more.

This was the Patrick who had first caught my interest—the Patrick who wasn't trying to hold back parts of himself, afraid that if he let someone else hold them, they might break. I pinned his wrists to the ground and felt him flex beneath me as our kiss deepened.

Patrick was strong. Stronger than he knew. He wasn't the kind of man who broke that easily—although, as his legs wrapped around my waist, I still wasn't sure how rough with him I wanted to be.

"Royce," Patrick gasped, breaking our kiss breathlessly. "Royce … there's something you should know about me."

I paused, hovering over him and smoothing his hair away from his forehead with my fingertip. "Tell me, then."

"I'm … I'm a virgin," he admitted softly. Like it was some kind of a bad thing. "I mean, I've done some stuff here and there, but…"

"Yeah. I figured as much." A wicked smile crossed my lips. "Did you really think I was about to take you in a manly fashion, right here in the snow?"

"It would be a very caveman-like thing to do," he pointed out.

I kissed the tip of his nose, then each cheek just below his long, dark eyelashes. "I'm not looking for caveman business here, Patrick. Well—I am, maybe, but not like that."

I kissed his jawline, then his ear, warming each place I kissed with the heat of my lips. "I need something real. Something with depth and value. You showed me that, actually."

"Keep kissing me like that," Patrick purred, "and I'll show you something that *really* has some depth."

"Mm … virginal, but horny." I ran my thumb over his lower lip, enjoying the way he felt beneath me in the frosted-over grass and snow. "Do you want me, Patrick?"

He let out a ragged breath, hugging my waist tighter with his legs. I could feel his cock, hard and eager, pressing against mine through our jeans. If I moved just so, I could work my bulge against his. Stroke him slightly, just by rubbing up against him.

As I did it, he gasped even harder. "I want you so fucking bad," he admitted. "So bad, it aches."

"If you want to stop, just say the word," I told him with a wolfish gaze. Then, pausing only to give him one final moment to think it over, I kissed him again.

His lips tasted like coffee and need. Our tongues tangled together, slick and desperate, seeking each other's warmth. I smoothed my hands down his chest, taking inventory of the exact way his body felt beneath mine. When my fingers found his waistband, they twisted the front button of his jeans open and yanked the zipper down with force.

It was just cold enough out that as I pulled his cock from his boxers and moved between his thighs, I could see my breath steam around his hard, thick length. He had a gorgeous cock, perfectly pink and throbbing. I lapped the pearl of precum off the tip of it, then ran my tongue around its head.

Patrick moaned, bucking his hips up to try to obtain more of that same pleasure. His fingers twisted into my hair with need.

"God," he gasped. "I've … I've never felt anything like that before."

"Like it?" I kissed his shaft, curling my fingers around the base.

He moaned. "The alphas I've been with before … I didn't think alphas were even into this."

I chuckled. "I'm not like other alphas, Patrick—so stop thinking about them. Right now, I want you to focus on me. On this. On how it makes you feel."

It was true. I wanted to make Patrick feel good, and I wanted to do it slowly enough that he could really relish it. I wanted to make him experience every sensation, enjoy it and adjust to it, before I moved onto the next.

Still, his cock was too hard to deny, and I was too hungry for it. I lost control of myself before I knew it, gulping him down and swallowing him whole. He came with a gasping moan that echoed through the clearing, filling my mouth with his hot, salty cum and shooting it down my throat.

"Want you," I growled, kissing him immediately after. I made him taste himself on my lips and tongue, which only made him moan even more.

"Let me use my mouth," he begged, pawing at the front of my jeans with his charcoal-stained fingers.

Now, I was too hard and too demanding to be quite so easy. So gentle. I stood, unzipping myself and taking his mouth while he knelt before me, kissing and sucking every bit of my cock he could get at. His lips slurped against the tip, wet and so hot that when he breathed out, the cold air all around us turned his breath into fog.

I was thicker, longer, and harder than most virgins ever expected—unless they were the kind of virgin who did their research watching a whole hell of a lot of porn—and as I claimed his mouth with my cock, smearing my precum across his tongue, I periodically had to stop to allow his jaw to adjust to my girth.

Still, Patrick was eager. His tongue slid up and down the underside of my shaft, slick and desperate to please. He was just as good with his lips when they were sucking as he was when they were kissing. With every thrust, I heard him coo and moan, high and sweet and hungry for more. His cold fingers curled beneath me, cupping the heat of my balls and massaging them gently. That sensation alone made me gasp and drive into him harder. Deeper.

I felt the need to come for him—come *inside him*—faster than I had expected. Before long, I was holding his head in mine and pumping thick, fertile ropes of my own cum down his throat and onto his tongue.

"More," he gasped, licking his lips and looking up at me wildly. "I want more."

I gave him a dark smile. "Tell me what you want, sweetheart."

"Fuck—fuck my ass, Royce. Take me—fucking *breed* me—"

He dove at my cock again, covering it with hungry kisses. It didn't surprise me in the least that I was already getting hard again. Patrick was fucking delicious, and there wasn't a thing he was begging for that I didn't want to give him.

But, with just enough sanity left to remember my vow, I pulled him to his feet and kissed his lips soothingly. "I want to," I told him. "I really do. But I don't have a condom on me—and we're taking things slow, remember?"

Patrick didn't even blush this time. He just stared up at me, still half-mad with longing, a smile on his perfect lips. "God, how I'm regretting those words now."

"You're so fucking good, sweetheart," I reassured him, turning his lips up to mine so I could kiss them again. "I have to admit, I'm tempted to take you—but you deserve better than to lose your virginity here in the woods. I know we'll both be happier if we wait."

"You're good to me, Royce," Patrick breathed against my lips. But as I pulled away slightly, I saw a fire burning in his forest-green eyes. "Just don't make me wait for long."

Chapter 10

Patrick

Tom called me out as soon as I came back in through the front door. "You *slut*," he cooed, sounding more impressed with me than I'd ever heard him.

"No. None of that from you." I shrugged my coat off and paused, giving him a quick look of interest. "Wait. How can you tell?"

"Because you don't look like you've got a stick up your ass for once. Who would have thought? All it took was another kind of stick to get it out of you."

"We didn't have sex, if that's what you're implying." I slipped my boots off and padded across the floor, still feeling pretty pleased with myself. "Which isn't to say that there wasn't any hanky panky, but…"

Tom roared with laughter, tossing his head back and clapping me on the shoulder as I walked by. "Hanky panky? Look at you, Pat! The only person I've ever heard talk like that is my omega grandpa, for fuck's sake. No wonder you're chasing an older man."

"He's chasing me, more like," I corrected him. "Not that I mind."

"Okay, okay. At least tell me this. Was it good?"

I paused in the archway to the kitchen, considering how much I actually wanted to reveal to Tom. "Very," I told him finally. "It was … beyond good."

"So you're seeing him again?"

I nodded, feeling the butterflies fluttering around in my stomach at the mere thought. "Yeah. Definitely. Soon, I hope."

As I fished around in the fridge for a piece of fruit to snack on before I headed to work, I realized that I couldn't stop smiling. I'd been so worried that Royce wouldn't understand my limits—that he'd push me like other alphas so often felt the need to do, or that he'd lose interest just because I wasn't putting out.

But not only had he waited until I was completely ready—in the end, it had been *me* who had wanted too much. Needed him too badly. I'd been perfectly ready to let Royce strip my pants off and fuck me there in the forest to the sound of the birds singing and the half-frozen waterfall. Little did he know that the waterfall was far from the only thing that had been gushing while I took his big, thick cock between my lips.

Fuck, I was horny today. I could feel it in the pleasant, tingling warmth between my legs and the way he'd left me lubricating and desperate. I could even feel it in my hips, the way they were gently easing outward in the hope that Royce's big, strong hands might be wrapped around them soon as he drove his cock into my tight, wet hole.

It was a damn good thing that Royce had such good control of himself, I realized. I'd even asked him to *breed* me, he'd had me so wanton and worked up. But Royce's self-control—and the lack of a condom—had saved me from getting knocked up as I lost my virginity in the forest, for which I was grateful.

Not that I exactly *minded* the idea of being knocked up by Royce—just, I knew that was probably just the horniness talking. So much for taking things slow, I guessed.

"Hey, Tom…" I walked back out into the living room and put on my most charming look. "After work, how would you feel about … I dunno, making yourself a little scarce for the evening."

"How scarce are we talkin'?" Tom grinned at me in a way that told me he knew exactly what I was asking for—the bastard was just making me say it.

"Politicians with morals scarce. I think I might invite Royce over after work, and…"

Tom's grin widened. "Say no more. I'll slink in sometime late tonight after you two have settled in for the evening—if I slink in at all. It's not right, you being the only one of us with a booty call for the evening."

"It's not a booty call," I grumbled as Tom rose, moving past me. "We're … well, at least I think we're exclusive. It's not like there's no preamble here."

"Call it what you like, bud." Tom snatched the half-eaten apple out of my hand and bit into it, claiming it for himself as he headed back to his room. "I'm just glad you're finally getting *laid*."

That night, after work, I let Royce in through the front door with a smile. He was wearing a pair of faded designer blue jeans and a dark, elegant cashmere sweater that felt like heaven against my cheek as I leaned in for a hug.

But Royce wasn't willing to settle for just a hug. While his arms were still wrapped around me, he pulled me into a deliciously long, slow kiss.

"Show me your art," he whispered against my lips. "I want to see it for myself."

I wanted to tell him that my art was the last thing I'd called him over to see, but Royce wasn't the kind of man who was easy to deny. In more ways than one, as it turned out. Before I knew it, I found my fingers wrapped around his broad palm as I led him to my bedroom. I didn't know what was making my heart pound harder—the thought of being so close to getting Royce into my bed, or the thought of showing him the only thing I'd ever done that I was really passionate about.

More likely than not, it was a little bit of both.

"Patrick … these are incredible." Royce unrolled one of my finished sketches, an uncommonly provocative piece I'd banged out in the weeks since I'd first met him. I felt my cheeks burn hot pink as I felt Royce's gaze linger on the slender curve of the spine of a heavy-lidded omega with his eyes closed in ecstasy. Behind the omega, a broad-shouldered alpha loomed, looking half-wild with longing as his lips curled into a snarl.

I expected him to tease me for it—especially since the alpha looked a hell of a lot like Royce himself—but to my relief, he was focused on the form of the piece, not the content.

"Look at what you've done with the shading here," he said, pointing to the shadows around the omega's stiff, swollen cock. "This is good. And the line work…"

"You don't think it's too … erotic?"

Royce met my gaze with his amber eyes. "Are you asking me if it makes me want to fuck something, Patrick?"

I looked him up and down, taking in everything he was. Tall. Handsome. Powerful. And, beyond all odds, standing in my bedroom, looking at me like I was a delicious cut of meat and he was a wolf at my door.

"Maybe not something…" I said softly. "But some*one*, on the other hand…"

I didn't need to say anything more.

Royce let the sketch roll back up. He dropped it back onto my desk, then moved toward me with hunger in his gaze. The way his body pressed against mine felt deliberate. Calculated. Like he was sizing me up, figuring out exactly how to take me.

By the time his lips found mine again, it seemed he'd decided on an approach: *Hard.*

Our fingers scrambled at the hems of each other's clothing, unzipping zippers, popping buttons, pulling shirts overhead and tossing them across the room onto the floor. He smelled like fresh linen and spearmint. As our bodies moved against each other, his scent mixed with the cedar and juniper of my cologne. We tumbled into bed together, tongues entwined and fingertips smoothing over each other's skin.

Royce's grip found my hips, my jaw. He positioned me as he liked, making me whimper with need. My own hormones were flooding my system with every kiss. Every touch. I wanted in him in ways that I'd never realized I could want a man.

I'd felt attraction before, sure. I'd felt desire. But none of it held a candle to the way I wanted Royce just then. None of it even came close.

He pushed me onto my back and rolled between my thighs. I laid back on the pillows, my breaths coming in ragged and sharp. His mouth was hot as he kissed my hips, my pelvis and finally, the precum-slickened tip of my cock. As he took me between his lips, his tongue was even hotter.

But when his mouth moved lower, licking at my balls and then at the tight pucker of my ass, his kisses almost felt cool compared to my own heat.

"You want me," he growled, forcing my legs further apart. "That's why you wanted me here tonight, wasn't it?"

"Yes," I admitted with a gasp. It felt so fucking good to spread my legs for Royce. My hips felt liquid, rolling in their joints like molten mercury. My whole body burned with need. "Earlier ... I wanted you so bad, Royce. I want you even more now."

"Good." He growled again as his tongue rimmed my asshole. He tasted my honey with a low, pleased moan. "Just remember—you asked for this."

"How could I forget," I breathed—then Royce's fingers claimed my ass, and that breath turned into a desperate gasp.

He pressed his index finger into me, then his middle finger as well. Royce worked slowly, but with a talented ferocity that told me he knew exactly what he was doing. He stroked my prostate, sending pangs of hot pleasure rolling through my body, then pressed deeper still. I heard the crinkle of a condom wrapper as Royce explored me, hooking his fingers upward.

He wasn't fingering my ass anymore—he was fingering the secondary channel in which we both truly wanted him to be. "Tell me you want it," he commanded. "Tell me what you need."

"I need you, Royce," I responded immediately—and my hips responded as well. With every twitch of his fingers, my hips bucked up to meet him almost involuntarily. "I need your cock—I need your thickness, your length."

"You want me to take you, don't you, Patrick?"

I nodded, biting my lip as Royce withdrew his fingers. He lapped at them, tasting me again, before he stroked my honey onto his condom-covered cock.

"I want you to take me," I told him. "I want you to take me *now*."

"If it hurts, we stop," he reassured me as his tip teased my hole.

He didn't look like he was going to want to stop, though. Good—I didn't want him to. But it was reassuring to know that he wanted me to enjoy it. That he cared about how I felt.

Somehow, I didn't think enjoying it was going to be a problem. Not with Royce between my thighs.

With a final nod from me, I could feel him giving into his own desires. He pressed into me, stretching my hole for him once more. But this time, it wasn't his fingers that were claiming me. It was his cock, stretching me open. Forcing the tightness of my hole to spread for him, to accommodate his girth. For a moment, it was almost uncomfortable, considering how huge he was.

He must have seen that on my face. Just a few inches in, he paused. "Shhh. I've got you," he soothed, pressing a kiss to my lips. "You okay?"

"Keep going," I begged him. Already, my body was adjusting to him.

He took me slowly at first, kissing my collarbones as he sank deeper into me. His hard, hairy body moved against mine with a controlled, measured need.

He was holding himself back. Forcing himself to be gentle. Sweet.

"Kiss me," I asked on a breath.

He was quick to comply. I closed my eyes, feeling his lips move sensually against my own. Porn hadn't prepared me for this. I wasn't sure anything could have.

In the darkness behind my eyelids, I felt like I was slipping into something more akin to a dream than reality. The bed creaked beneath us, rocking softly against the wall as it bore our weights. Above me, Royce's body covered me completely, driving throb after throb of dark, rich pleasure through my core with every thrust.

Gradually, Royce picked up the pace. He wasn't fucking me slowly anymore. He was fucking me hard, fast, halfway between ruthlessness and making love. His arms wrapped around me, pulling my body closer against his own. He used his hold on me as leverage to thrust even harder, even deeper, until his cock bottomed out against my cervix.

"Kiss me," I begged him, gasping. The sensation was intense and all-consuming, hot like pleasure, a bit sharp like pain. "Kiss me again."

I needed his lips, and he gave them to me without hesitation. Our bodies rolled in bed together as our mouths met. I tasted salt and iron, the faintest hint of apple pie on his tongue.

When the kiss finally broke, I was on top of him. Riding him. Showing him exactly how deep I wanted him, how truly desperate for his cock I could be.

This new position let me set the pace, but it also gave Royce access to my chest and my own cock. He ran a thumb across my nipple, then pinched it between his fingers until I moaned and drove him into me even harder.

He was getting close, I could tell. So was I. But as if the sensations he was giving me at the end of his cock weren't already overwhelming enough, Royce wrapped his fist around my own throbbing dick.

"Come with me," he commanded. "Give it to me, Patrick."

"I want to," I whimpered. "God … I really do. I need you—I'm yours—"

"Then come, Patrick." His eyes were dark and hooded, like he was daring me to find out what would happen it I disobeyed. "Come with me—give yourself to me! Come, Patrick! Come!"

My balls tightened at his command. As my ass did the same, I felt his cock twitch within me, preparing to pump the condom full of his cum. I whimpered. Royce grunted, then let out a low moan.

It was an orgasm in three parts: the one inside me, throbbing and wet and electric; the one in my cock, bursting with semen that rained down on Royce's chest; and Royce's own orgasm, deep inside me, filling me up and making me whole.

His lips were still pulled back in a snarl, but Royce looked satisfied. Spent. He rolled us over, and as he looked down at me, the snarl shifted into a soft smile. It took me a second to realize it was because he was looking at the smile playing on my own lips.

Royce dropped himself down onto his elbows, pressing his sweat-slickened chest against mine. His tongue lapped at my neck, and then a growl emanated from his throat as he sank his teeth gently into my collarbone.

"Mine," he grunted, an animalistic afterthought.

"Yours," I cooed softly beneath him, enjoying the slickness of his body. The warmth of his cum, still buried so deep inside me.

We laid there for a long time just like that, synchronizing our breathing. Bathing in each other's pleasure.

"How was it?" he asked at last, covering me with kisses as I cuddled against him.

I laughed, relaxing against his warmth. "That was the most intense thing I've ever felt."

"Good. That's how it should feel."

"And it's like that every time?"

He chuckled. "Maybe not with everyone—but with me, it always will be."

"Wow," I said softly, pressing my cheek against his chest. I felt small and safe and happy in his arms. All I wanted to do now was curl up against him, breathing in his musk, the wintery smell of his deodorant, and that faint scent of hops he carried in his hair as I fell asleep. "Wow."

Royce's cock slipped from my ass, feeling sticky with what I assumed was an insane amount of my honey as it slid against my thigh.

But then Royce made a displeased grunt. "Fuck," he swore. "Patrick … we may have a problem."

"Oh god." I immediately blushed. Had I done something wrong? "What happened? What did I do?"

"Not you," Royce assured me. "The condom."

I raised myself up so I could glance down at Royce's cock. The condom was split down the middle, covered in about half of his load.

The other half, I presumed, was still inside me.

I looked down at him, a tinge of fear snaking down my spine. "Oh no."

Chapter 11

Royce

Two weeks later, I was still playing every moment of that night with Patrick over in my head.

"What's got you so fucking twitchy?" Cam asked, after watching me dive across my desk for my phone for the third time that day.

I checked the message—just a quick text from Patrick letting me know he was headed to brunch with Thomas. It warmed me straight through to see the little "xx" he tacked on at the end of the message, but Cam's question reminded me of exactly how antsy I'd been since the condom incident. I'd made myself available 24/7, just in case Patrick needed anything or started showing signs of morning sickness.

I knew that Patrick was on high alert, too. Maybe even more so than I was.

"Too much coffee, I guess." I answered Cam's question without even looking up from my phone. I considered telling him the truth, but my attention was already too split to get an earful from Cam on top of it.

Don't let Tom talk you into any mimosas, I warned Patrick via text.

Only virgin screwdrivers for me, he sent back.

Patrick had been quick to lay down a few ground rules for himself after we'd realized the condom had broken—no drinking among them. I'd taken the same vow until we knew for sure that there wasn't a little Wheeler growing in Patrick's womb.

So when Cam slid me his latest mystery beer concoction, I had to (not so unhappily) decline.

"Come on, man. It's a tequila-aged white-blonde lager. This could be our next big thing come summer!"

"I'd prefer to focus on our current big thing." I pushed the glass of beer back at him. "We still need a name before we even start to talk bottle art, and frankly, even then I'm not sure we're going to be ready in time."

"Is that what this newfound sobriety thing is about?" Cam looked down at his new beer with disappointment. "Alcohol is supposed to enhance your creativity, you know…"

"I'll be okay. It's good to shake things up a little bit." And nothing shook things up more than potentially becoming a father, right?

"You texting Patrick?" Cam asked, as my phone buzzed again.

Wanna swing by my place for a movie tonight?

I smirked down at my phone. *You gonna let me pick the film if I do?*

"Hello … Earth to Royce? Come in, Royce."

I glanced up at Cam, who looked a mix of concerned and annoyed. "Yeah, I'm texting Patrick. He's grabbing brunch with Thomas. Might head over to his place for a movie later."

"So things are going well, then?" Cam crossed his arms over his chest and raised an eyebrow.

For a second time that day, I considered telling him. Cam and I were far from the kind of brothers who shared everything—except boyfriends, apparently—but I didn't like lying, regardless of why the lie was being told. It almost felt wrong *not* telling him, in fact.

But out of all my current worries and excitements, hearing my little brother tell me how irresponsible I was being for potentially knocking up a twenty-five-year-old omega was ranking pretty low on my list of ways to spend the afternoon. I wanted to tell Cam, but for the moment, the timing wasn't right. Plus, there was still a chance that the whole thing would turn out to be a non-issue when Patrick took his pregnancy test in a few days—and it didn't seem fair to Patrick to go airing his dirty laundry to his ex without his permission.

"Things are going … better than well," I finally said. It wasn't a lie—not even close. "Patrick's a great guy, so I'm not surprised … but honestly, I've never enjoyed a relationship this much before."

At that, Cam smiled. "You know, I thought it would be weird, you dating my ex and all. But now that I've seen you two together, it's kind of warming my cold little heart. You seem good for each other—and he's definitely not the kind of guy to go fucking around on you."

"He's completely unlike anyone I've ever dated," I mused. "Maybe that's why."

Cam grinned and clapped me on the shoulder. "Looks good on you, man. I'm really happy for you guys."

"Thanks," I told him. "Means a lot."

Cam raised the glass of beer he'd poured for me in a silent toast, then took a big swig of it. From the way his face turned a little green as the beer hit his tongue, it was obvious that the new brew wasn't exactly the winner he'd been hoping for.

I should have recognized a bad omen when I saw one. But as Cam ran to the sink to spit the beer out, and the brewery's front door swung open, it was already too late.

"Royce?"

I looked up from the table that Cam and I had turned into my marketing work station, secretly hoping to see Patrick's face. It wouldn't have been the first time he'd done that—told me he was going one place, then showed up at the brewery with some coffee and a pie instead. I loved little surprises like that, and Patrick had been the first guy I'd ever dated to actually pick up on it.

Seeing Brendan standing in the doorway of my brother's brewery definitely wasn't the kind of surprise I appreciated.

But seeing him standing in that doorway wearing a wool overcoat and a pink cashmere crop-top, revealing a baby bump?

I suddenly wished I'd taken Cam up on his offer of a beer.

"Brendan … what are you doing here?" I tried not to sound too accusatory in my tone, but I fucking failed. Not just because Brendan Marquette, the man who had fucked my boss and fucked over my life in the process, was the last person I wanted to see right now—but because I knew what he was going to say to me next before he even opened his mouth.

It didn't stop him from saying it anyway, though. The words came out, like I knew they would, each more horrible than the last.

"Royce … I love you," he told me, pulling the door closed behind him. "I miss you. I want you. And believe it or not … I'm pregnant." Brendan caressed his belly as he gave me a soft smile. "You're going to be a father."

Just then, a retch came from Cam back in the kitchen. When he pulled his head up out of the sink and looked at Brendan across the bar, there was a sneer on his lips. "Like *hell* he is!" Cam yelled.

Brendan's eyes narrowed as he glanced between Cam and me. "Royce … I think this might need to be a conversation you and I have *alone.*"

Chapter 12

Patrick

"Did you tell him?" Tom asked as we left the pharmacy with our purchases. Tom's was his birth control. Mine was something just as important.

"I told him that we were doing brunch."

Tom scowled at me, then bopped me on the back of the head with his palm. "You should have invited him over, dummy! And that delicious brother of his too, for that matter. I could have made virgin martinis—which would have been ironic, considering…"

"Considering that I'm not a virgin anymore?" I rolled my eyes. "Believe me, the irony isn't lost on me, Tom."

"So message him back. Tell him what you're really up to. We can swing by the craft store for some confetti and streamers. Throw you a proper party and everything."

My shoulders slumped forward as I shook my head. "We're not throwing a party to celebrate me peeing on a stick."

"And why the hell not?"

I laughed at Tom's outrage. "No wonder alphas think omegas are so extra. Let's just get home so we can do this, okay?"

"Are you excited?" Tom asked.

We climbed up into my truck and buckled our seat belts. I took a deep breath, feeling the mix of excitement and nausea churning in my stomach. "Yeah," I admitted. "Scared, but excited, too. It's a weird mix."

"What about Royce? Any idea where he's at on any of this?"

I laughed again as I put the truck into gear. "He's all too eager to be helpful right now, I think. I can barely shoot him a simple text without getting a reply a few seconds later."

Tom glanced down at his phone, which hadn't buzzed all morning. "You lucky bastard." Still, when he looked back up at me, he was grinning. "Royce so wants you to be preggo. It's adorable."

"I don't know about that."

"Did you tell him about the morning sickness, at least?"

I shook my head. "It might not even be morning sickness. It might be … I don't know. Stress. Or nerves."

"Or maybe you just need a healthy dose of Royce's dick again."

"And risk another broken condom?" I bit my lip as I pulled out of the parking lot. I didn't want to admit it, but just the thought of having Royce inside me again—condom or no—was enough to make my heart skip a hopeful beat. "Maybe you're right."

Tom let out a celebratory whoop. He drummed on the dash in excitement. "I knew it! Fucking knew it. You *do* want Royce's babies! Knew it all along."

I tried not to smile, but it was too hard to hold it back. Since that night with Royce, I'd been getting more and more certain that he really had knocked me up— and as scared as I was about being right about it, I was also kind of hoping it wasn't a false alarm.

Royce had made me feel wanted. Safe. I was more myself with him than I'd ever felt.

With the rush of weird side effects that I'd been going through—not just the morning sickness, but a heightened sense of smell and a few weird cravings—that fact was ringing more true than ever. The world seemed to have more colors in it now. Everything tasted so much better, and my emotions were so much bolder and brighter.

But at the same time, I couldn't help reminding myself that this wouldn't all be fun and games if I turned out to be pregnant with Royce's child. Our relationship was still so new and unexplored. Royce's last relationship had only just ended a month ago, and his time in Carter's Crossing had an expiration date.

Even if he *did* want the baby, and he *did* stay, I had plenty of baggage of my own to deal with. Would I really be able to run my dad's diner while pregnant? Was I really ready to be a father? Was he?

"Okay, princess. Stop worrying—that's an order." Tom turned in his seat and gave me a serious look. "No matter what happens, Royce has been nothing but supportive. And even if he changes his mind about that, you've got your dad and me to depend on. You're not going to have to go through this alone."

I made sure to honk before I took the turn around Devil's Bend. Thomas was right in that regard—no matter what happened, I knew that things would turn out okay.

It wasn't the result that was giving me nerves, I realized. It was just the anticipation. Knowing meant that I could start planning for the future. Not knowing left everything up in the air completely.

"Guess there's no time like the present to find out." I pulled the truck up to the apartment that Tom and I shared. "But if it's a no, I expect a martini on stand-by. Gin, if we've got it."

"Please." Tom rolled his eyes as he hopped out of the truck. "Like I would live in a place that wasn't stocked with a bottle of good gin."

I emerged from our bathroom a few minutes later, anxiously wiggling the little plastic wand that would tell me my fate. "Well?" Tom asked.

"We've gotta give it a minute still."

"Okay. Cool. I've prepared *two* drinks for you, then. Just in case." Tom turned to the counter, picking up a drink in each hand and raising them in demonstration. "Left is a virgin, right has the strong stuff."

We waited in silence for a few moments as the test finished processing. "So? You're killing me here, man!"

I grinned, taking the drink on the left.

"Yes!" Tom clinked the rim of the other martini glass against mine and tossed his drink back victoriously. "I knew it! I fucking *knew* it!"

"Next time, I'll just ask you, then." I suppressed my grin for just long enough to sip on my virgin martini. It didn't taste like much, but I didn't mind.

Everything I'd felt over the last few weeks had been real. The morning sickness, the sensitivity, the way my entire emotional spectrum had shifted from a gentle prelude to an entire gospel choir of activity—it was all confirmed at the sight of those two little blue lines.

Pregnant. I was going to have Royce's baby.

"Come on." Tom grabbed my keys and headed for the door, pausing only to pour himself another slosh of gin. "We've gotta go tell him. Like, immediately."

"Not so fast there, drinky." I snatched the keys from him before he got any more bright ideas. "You stay here and celebrate on my behalf—I want to tell him myself."

Tom pouted, but another sip of his drink seemed to sort out his disappointment. "You just want him to give you a victory fuck when you tell him, don't you?"

"Maybe I do." I grinned, hugged Tom, and headed for the door. "And maybe he will."

"Tell him congrats for me!" Tom yelled after me. "Tell him I'm gonna be an uncle!"

I didn't have the heart to tell Tom that wasn't how uncles worked. If the boy wanted to be an uncle, as far as I was concerned, he was welcome to it. With the way the excitement of it all was making my head spin, I'd need all of the help I could get—familial or otherwise. Which reminded me—I'd need to tell my omega dad. I'd need to tell the staff at the diner. Probably, at some point, I'd need to tell Cam.

But most of all, before anything else…I'd need to tell Royce. My omega dad had waited three weeks to tell my alpha dad that he was pregnant with me. I'd even heard of some omegas who didn't tell their alphas about a pregnancy until as late as the end of the first trimester. As I headed for my truck, I didn't think I could wait that long. Tom's enthusiasm had been infectious, and Royce's attentiveness warranted some reward.

At least, I hoped Royce would see it as a reward. The last thing I wanted was to strap him with bad news. If anything, I wanted to give Royce something to look forward to.

I was halfway to the brewery before it even occurred to me that maybe Royce wouldn't be happy to hear the big news. Maybe he'd been keeping such good tabs on me since our little slip with the condom because a baby was exactly what he was hoping against.

As I pulled up to Big Hops, I put those notions from my mind. For better or worse, I was having Royce's baby now. He deserved the right to know that I was pregnant with his child. Whatever happened after that, I knew that I would get through it…

But as I imagined holding a tiny hand in mine three years down the road or so as I took our little toddler to see their alpha daddy at work, I couldn't help but hold out the hope that Royce would react positively to the news. Maybe it was just the hormones talking, but I could really see myself starting a family with Royce. Maybe even marriage, somewhere down the line. We hadn't known each other for long, but life had a way of pushing people together like that—especially here in Carter's Crossing.

The anticipation of having my entire future on the line, depending on how the next few minutes played out, had my heart racing. I paused at the brewery's front door just before I pushed it open to catch my breath.

That's when I saw them. A pregnant omega wearing a pink crop top, and Royce, out in the middle of the brewery's reception area. The omega had his hands on his hips. Royce's own arms were settled across his chest. They looked like they were having a serious conversation—and something told me it had a lot to do with the baby bump currently gracing the omega's abdomen.

It took me a moment, but I was able to recognize the omega. Not anyone local, thank god—it was Brendan, Royce's ex. I'd seen him in a few of Royce's pictures from their trip to Italy together. He was handsome enough and distinct enough that his face was easy to remember.

Now that I was seeing him standing there in front of the father of my child, running his hand over a pregnant belly of his own, I doubted it was a face I'd ever be able to forget.

Immediately, I felt it. The shock of all my silly little dreams crashing down around me. If Brendan was pregnant, and had come all the way to Carter's Crossing to confront Royce, there was only one possible reason why: he thought he was having Royce's baby too.

But could that even be possible? Brendan looked a few months along, and Royce had only been here in Carter's Crossing for around a month, so the timing would work out.

If it had been anyone else who had gotten me pregnant, I would have left then and there. I had plenty of opinions about alphas who went around knocking up any omega they could get their cock into. I'd heard the sad stories from some of my friends about alphas who liked to sow their wild oats with as many omegas as possible, only to bounce when faced with any concept of responsibility.

But Royce wasn't like that. Royce had respected my boundaries. He'd treated me well. And in the days leading up to me finally taking the pregnancy test, he'd been nothing but attentive.

I decided to wait it out. After all he'd done for me, Royce deserved the benefit of the doubt.

I ran my hands over my own stomach as I walked back to my truck. Royce wasn't the only one who deserved a little patience here, I realized. It wasn't just my own fears I had to worry about now. The life of the child growing inside me deserved the chance of having a full set of parents too. I knew too well what it was like growing up with only one father. I wanted my baby to have the opportunity of having the life I'd never been able to have.

All I could do was wait now. Wait, and wonder … and hope.

Chapter 13

Royce

"Paternity test." I said the words, crisp and clear, before Brendan could spin me any more of his special brand of bullshit. "I don't want to hear any more about this until I know for sure that this baby is mine."

Brendan stuck his lower lip out, immediately broadcasting how victimized he felt by that demand. "Of course it's yours! Who else's would it be, Royce?"

"Don's, for one." I held my ground, not allowing myself to fall into one of Brendan's infamously well-laid emotional traps. "And who even knows what other men you were sleeping with behind my back. Could be half the alphas in Manhattan, for all I know."

"Royce … don't be like this. You know we wanted this … you know we were trying. And look."

Brendan smoothed his hands over his swelling belly, looking up at me with the same pleading gaze he'd given me when I'd caught him with my boss' dick in his ass. "Now it's finally happening. You're going to be a daddy, Royce. Isn't this exactly what you wanted?"

I stifled my reaction. Even the slightest shift in my expression would urge Brendan to stay the course on this, and I didn't want to give him the satisfaction of knowing that he was getting to me. Not until I could be sure myself.

"I wanted a partner who I could trust not to cheat on me with the first alpha who so much as looked his way, Brendan. If you're happy to be having this baby, then I'm happy for you—but given your track record, I think it's understandable why I would have my doubts that it has anything to do with me."

"You *bred* me, Royce! You fucked me without a condom! I don't understand why it's is so hard for you to put two and two together on this!"

"Then get me a paternity test," I told him again. "Prove to me that this isn't just another one of your lies, and we'll talk."

The non-reactive thing finally panned out. Seeing that he wasn't going to appeal to my bleeding heart or my guilt, Brendan shifted tactics. He went from pouting and *poor me* to sensual and sultry in an instant, taking a few steps toward me until he could lay his hands on my chest and give me his best bedroom eyes.

"I'll get the test," he promised. "I'll do anything you want, Royce. As long as we can be together again. I've missed you so much…"

"I'm sure."

"And I regret anything I might have done to hurt you…"

"That's very generous of you."

"But I'm ready to put the past behind us now. I want to be yours again—I want us to be a *family*, Royce. Isn't that what you've always wanted?"

It was then that I made my mistake, glancing over Brendan's shoulder at my phone on the table. He was right—I *had* always wanted a family. My own fathers had raised Dana, Camden and me in the most loving environment I could have ever imagined, and deep in my heart, I knew that I wanted to carry on the tradition. The Wheelers were a family-oriented clan, and I was long overdue for my chance to start my own branch of the family tree.

But I already had something potentially budding for me in the family way— and it wasn't with someone so faithless and conniving as the man standing before me, simpering and stroking my chest like I was some kind of dog who could be lured away from my own best interests with the promise of a tasty treat. My relationship with Brendan had always left a bad taste in my mouth—and in that moment, my mind wasn't focused on the past anymore.

It was Patrick I wanted. He'd made me slow down and reconsider the way I was living my life. Patrick was the one who'd given me hope for a relationship where I didn't have to worry about where my partner was, or who he was fucking when I wasn't around.

But Brendan saw my eyes glance at my phone, and he snapped up that tiny reaction like bait on the line.

"Don't look away from me, you monster!" His palms on my chest turned to fists, pounding against my pectorals in frustration. "You strapped me with this baby and then you left the fucking state, Royce! Is that the kind of man you are?

"When we first got together, I knew you were the love 'em and leave 'em type, but I *believed* in you, dammit! I believed that I could change you—I saw something in you that *no one else* had ever seen before, and I—"

"Paternity test," I said again, meeting him with yet another impassive gaze. "You moved on long before I left the city, Brendan. I've moved on, too."

"Is that so?" Brendan sneered. "Who is he, then? Some backwoods country slut, huh? Is that what you've been doing out here—shacking up with some classless little whore who doesn't know about you and your playboy ways?"

"I think you should go back to the city," I told Brendan honestly. "New York is better suited for your dramatics. Get me a paternity test that proves this child is even mine, and I'll make sure you're taken care of—but until I have proof, I don't see how this is my problem."

It felt cold to say those words. It left a twisted knot of self-loathing in my stomach to see the look on Brendan's face once they were said. But if I didn't say them now, I knew things would only be worse for the both of us.

I didn't love Brendan anymore. As much as Brendan had hurt me, I'd been cheated on too many times, by him and men like him, to fall into this kind of trap.

Men like Brendan were toxic. Insidious. They preyed upon men like me, men they knew would always try to do the right thing, no matter the personal cost—and it was all too easy to fall into the trap.

I could believe Brendan. I could accept the responsibility of his child, go back to the city with him, and return to a life that I knew would make me miserable, just to avoid feeling like an asshole while he confronted me with what was, more likely than not, just the latest flavor in his cocktail of lies.

But what kind of life would that be for either of us if I did? What kind of life would that be for the child he was carrying? And where would that leave Patrick—the only man who'd ever made me feel like maybe there could be something more to a relationship than the constant barrage of drama and uncertainties I'd experienced?

"You're a bastard, Royce Wheeler," Brendan spat at me.

"I'm a man of my word," I countered. "Paternity test, or we're done here."

Brendan drew back, obviously perplexed. I'd fended off every other form of emotional manipulation on his part so far, and I could tell that he was struggling to find a new angle on this.

It surprised me a little, honestly. Normally, Brendan's bag of tricks ran a little deeper than this. Maybe this baby really was mine—or maybe, he was just losing his touch.

"I'm not leaving until you own up to what you've done to me, Royce."

"I think you'd be happier sorting this out in the city. If you need money for gas, I'll go get my wallet."

"Oh, no. You're not getting rid of me *that* easily." Brendan huffed indignantly. "Besides, I've already booked a room here for a few days. I need the fresh air … almost as badly as I need you."

"I don't want drama, Brendan," I warned him, seeing the seductive look in his eyes again. "And if you give a damn about your baby, neither should you."

Immediately, Brendan's brow lowered into a scowl. "*Our* baby, you asshole." He reached toward me again, and for a moment, I thought he was going to try to kiss me. Instead, he reached up and plucked a hair from my head, holding it up in grim triumph.

"You want proof? I'll get you proof. Don't think you've heard the last of us. We *will* be a family again—whether you like it or not. Tell your country slut to start packing his bags."

I watched him storm out, slamming the door behind him.

"All clear?" Cam peeked his head out from the office behind the bar as soon as we heard Brendan's car peel out of the parking lot.

"For now."

"Good," Cam said. "Because … well, I don't know how to tell you this, but Patrick's truck is out in the parking lot."

Dealing with Brendan had left my stomach tied up in knots, but at the slightest mention of Patrick, my guts untangled themselves immediately and my heart swelled with hope and joy.

Patrick. If he was here, and he hadn't called … it could only mean one thing.

There was something he wanted to tell me. Something that could only be said in person. Whether it was good news or bad, I didn't care—I was just happy to see him again.

The door of his truck swung open, and he hopped down from it as I came out the brewery's front door.

"Hey," he said softly, giving me a little wave.

"Hey," I said back, slowing to a stop a few feet away from him in the parking lot. It felt like there was something between us, something with more depth and importance than anything Brendan could have dragged back from the city to lay at my feet.

Our future. Good news or bad … pregnant or not.

He tossed me something slender and white before I could even figure out how to ask. I caught it and turned it over in my hands excitedly. Holding my breath, I stared down at two little blue lines in the window of the pregnancy test.

"Two lines…" I said softly, staring down at him as my heart flooded with hope. "That means…"

"I'm pregnant, Royce." Patrick nodded, biting his lower lip. "I know this might not be the best of times, but…"

I closed the gap between us immediately, wrapping my arms around him and pulling him into the kind of kiss that stifled any apology that might have been brewing behind his perfect lips.

"Your timing couldn't have been better," I promised him, unable to control my grin. "I'm going to be a dad?"

Patrick's lips eased into a smile of his own. "You're going to be a dad, Royce."

And in that moment, I knew. No matter what, my future was standing right in front of me. It would be me, Patrick, and the little life that was stirring in his belly between us.

No matter what.

Chapter 14

Patrick

The gravel of the parking lot crunched beneath our feet as we kissed. From the way Royce's lips moved against mine, I could tell immediately that he was all in. Royce was like that—all or nothing.

I'd known it from the moment he'd first accepted my terms of courtship. If a man with a playboy reputation like Royce's could change his approach so completely, then there wasn't anything he'd let stand between him and what he wanted.

But if he wanted me ... we had more than a few things to work out first.

For a moment, though, I let myself enjoy him. I tasted the comfort of his lips. I let his hands move over my body, soothing my muscles and easing my anxieties away.

It felt incredible to be touched like that. It always had. But now, with all of these hormones coursing through my veins and amplifying every sensation, it felt even better.

I only wished it could have lasted.

"Why didn't you come in and tell me?" Royce asked, trying to tease me. "I can't believe you made me trudge out here to the parking lot just to hear the big news."

"I, ah … I saw you and Brendan arguing inside," I told him honestly. "That was him, wasn't it?"

Royce drew away slightly, a furrow in his brow. "It was. What did you hear?"

"Nothing. It just … it didn't seem right. I thought I'd wait until he left to come in and tell you. When you came out, I was still working up the nerve."

Which wasn't entirely true. I'd needed to brace myself before I told Royce about my pregnancy, of course, but I didn't tell him why.

He wouldn't be the first alpha who'd lied to me about his ideas of commitment. Since meeting him, I'd hoped those days would be long gone … but now, with Brendan in the picture again, there was no way to be sure.

"You don't have to worry about my ex, Patrick. That's water under the bridge now." His fingertips brushed against my stomach, hesitating over the place where we both knew our child was growing just beneath his touch. "This is what matters to me. You, me, and this baby. Everything else is secondary. Okay?"

His amber eyes were honest and hopeful, but my fears were still coiling in my stomach, heavy and dark.

"Want to go grab something to eat?" I asked, hoping that I could treat those fears like hunger and eat them away.

Royce smirked. "Pregnancy cravings already, huh?"

I couldn't help it—I smiled back. "I've been having the weirdest desire to eat fried chicken and maple syrup all morning."

His smirk widened into a grin. "Chicken and waffles at that organic place on Main, then. Come on—I'll drive."

The chicken and waffles satisfied my cravings, although they were replaced with newer, weirder ones by the time I was halfway through my plate. Royce didn't bring up talk of the future until he'd settled me with a chocolate milkshake and a plate of french fries as well.

But no matter how much I ate, the feeling of uncertainty and dread seemed to remain.

"I've got a place in the city," he offered. His fingertips brushed idly against mine as I reached for another fry. "Big, beautiful lofted penthouse. You'd love it there. I've even got a couple of spare rooms that I've been in the process of remodeling. We could turn one into a studio … one into a nursery."

I could see the stars in Royce's eyes as he spoke. There was no denying that Royce seemed entirely caught up in the magic of all this new potential between us. It was hard not to get caught up in it right along with him.

A penthouse in the big city, a safe place to raise our baby, and a studio for my art? A few months ago, I would have killed for an offer like that. But now that I was actually being faced with it, things were proving to be a little more complicated.

"That sounds incredible," I admitted. "It's just…"

"Too good to be true?" Royce, laughed, stealing a fry. "Believe it, Patrick. We can make this happen. All the groundwork has already been laid—all that's missing right now is you."

"It's not quite that simple for me, though." It felt awkward that I even had to remind him. Not everyone's life could be so easily picked up and moved like Royce's apparently could be. My ties to Carter's Crossing ran deeper than his did.

"I have my dad's diner to think of, Royce—he wants to retire in a few months, and there's no one to leave it to but me."

"But you don't want to work at the Lonely Hearts for the rest of your life…" Something wasn't clicking with Royce. It was like he'd never had to do anything he hadn't wanted to do before.

"You're too big for this little town, Patrick. In the city, you can be anything you want to be. You want to do art? Become an artist, then. I have connections— you could paint for six months and have a gallery show in seven. Doesn't that sound like the kind of life you've always wanted for yourself?"

I sighed. "It *does*. I'm not going to pretend otherwise. But Carter's Crossing is my home. I have responsibilities here. I have people who depend on me. Don't pretend like this is an easy decision when it's not."

Suddenly, I didn't even have appetite for the fries anymore, and the milkshake tasted all too sweet for my palate. If Royce couldn't understand why I wouldn't want to leave Carter's Crossing, then he didn't know me as well as I'd hoped.

But Royce was quick to see when he'd done wrong. The hurt was written all over his face. Part of it was probably the realization that the life he'd planned for us wasn't going to go as smoothly as he'd imagined it in his head, but as he took my hands in his, I could tell that it ran deeper than that, too.

"God. I'm an asshole," he said softly, bringing my knuckles to his lips and kissing them. "Of course you have responsibilities here, Patrick. I'm sorry for making you feel like I didn't care about them, or like I wasn't respecting them. I … I get a little too caught up in my plans sometimes. It takes a kick in the ass to remind me that not everything revolves around me and what I want."

"Old habits die hard, huh?" I teased with a little smirk. Royce was proving to be surprisingly easy to forgive.

"Not as hard as you think," he assured me. "I do want you in the city with me, Patrick. You'd love it there. I know you would. And as much as you downplay your artistic notions … they could become so much more than just dreams there.

"I want what's best for you. For us. For…" He smiled softly. "Do you think it'll be a boy or a girl?"

His smile was infectious. "It's too early to tell. Are you hoping one way or another?"

He shook his head. "Boy or girl—doesn't matter. As long as you're both healthy and mine. That's the important thing."

"Even if we're healthy and yours … and here?" My voice trembled with a worry that I didn't want to betray.

Royce sighed. "That's the thing, isn't it? These weeks I've spent here in Carter's Crossing have been life-changing." He glanced down at my stomach, then looked deeply into my eyes.

"In more ways than one. But I don't know that there's a life for me *here*, as much as I hate to admit it. There's not a lot of work for an over-educated marketing VP out here in the mountains. I could work at the brewery, I guess…"

I could already see Royce running numbers and making plans in his head. He was action-oriented like that. Always figuring out a plan of attack.

I liked that about him—he looked at any trouble that he was faced with, squared his shoulders, and was always ready to face it head on. Royce had his flaws, same as anyone—but cowardice wasn't among them.

That alone made him the kind of man I could see myself being with forever. The kind of man I could marry and raise a family with. It was a strange realization—simultaneously so exciting and so bittersweet.

There were two paths ahead of us now. Taking either could lead to a happy life for all three of us—this baby, Royce, and me. But both would require sacrifices that I wasn't sure either of us knew how to make.

On top of it all, Brendan's visit this morning was still looming over me like a thick, black storm cloud. I felt like Royce wasn't telling me everything about his conversation with Brendan. Hell, maybe it wasn't his story to tell. But all of it was clumping together like a massive snowball tumbling down the side of the mountain, and I still wasn't sure whether it would crush us beneath its weight or pass us by completely.

"We don't have to decide just now," I told him. Now it was my turn to press his knuckles to *my* lips.

"But we'll have to decide eventually," Royce said. "You think your end over, I'll consider mine?"

I kissed his fingers again before I rested our hands on the table between us. "Agreed."

Royce grinned. "In the meantime … let's just enjoy this for what it is, I say. Want to head over to the diner and tell your dad? I haven't had a chance to meet him properly yet, but he might be excited to learn that he's going to be a grandfather."

I wanted to tell him yes. I wanted to allow myself to fall into the same excited energy I saw reflected in his eyes, to give myself over to the joy of all the possibilities ahead of us.

But beneath that excitement, for me at least, there was still a lot of fear. I wasn't as brave as Royce. I still worried too much about all of these unknowns. And even if he decided to stay with me here, I wasn't sure I could ask that of him.

I wasn't sure that our story had a happy ending yet. And until I could be, I didn't want to complicate things any further than they already were.

"I'm actually feeling pretty tired," I half-lied. "My body's still adjusting to this whole pregnancy thing, and…"

"Say no more." Royce waved for the bill and offered me another fry, dangling it temptingly in front of my lips. "I'll drive you home so you can get some rest. Your keys in your truck?"

I nodded.

"Then Cam and I will drop it off back at your place later." Royce dipped the fry in the milkshake and offered it to me again.

Feeling the hunger in my stomach return, I forced a smile and leaned forward to take the fry between my lips. The rush of salty and warm, cold and sweet left all of my senses tingling in delight…

But beneath them, the fear still remained—and it would take a lot more than some satisfied pregnancy cravings and some ghosts of a plan to put them to rest.

Chapter 15

Royce

"Still not drinking?" Cam asked, pouring himself a cold pint of the still-unnamed lager.

I eyed the window, watching the snow dump down outside, and shook my head. "Coffee is doing me fine. It's cold enough out; wouldn't you rather have something warm?"

"And deny myself the pleasure of indulging myself like a complete asshole while you sit there all serious and sober?" Cam laughed and slid into a seat at our worktable. "Not on my life. How's everything coming?"

I wanted to tell him about Patrick—about the way thing were still up in the air between us, while Brendan's web of lies loomed on the horizon—but I knew it wasn't my love life that concerned Cam right now. It was the fate of his beer he wanted to hear about.

"Marketing plan." I slid the documents over for him to look at, one by one. "Distribution outlines. Contracts with our east coast partners—samples have been shipped already, and they're all loving it. Sounds like they'll be eager to have us on their shelves as soon as we're ready."

"They'd better be." Cam glanced down at the contracts, then pushed them away. "You know all this business-y shit is over my head—but I trust you, man. Not sure how I could have done this without you, actually."

I smiled. At least when it came to marketing, I still knew how to do something right. "In that case, all we've got left to worry about is—"

"Art," Cam groaned. "And the name. Fuck—why is naming something so damn hard?"

"Decision-making is the cross the businessman has to bear," I commiserated—though I wasn't exactly talking about the beer. "Any new contenders to add to the list?"

We both glanced at the white board where we'd been scrawling names for the last month. It had almost been turned completely black with options at this point. Unfortunately, options didn't matter so much when none of them were the right one.

"I say we just beg a knife off Patrick's dad and chuck it at the damn thing at this point. Whatever sticks, that's what we go with."

I snorted. "That's the worst business plan I've ever heard in my life. Didn't college teach you anything?"

"It did." Cam took a sip of his beer and wiped the foam from his upper lip. "It taught me that I'm just smart enough at business to get myself into trouble with it. Unfortunately, I had to get into the trouble to learn that college didn't teach me nearly enough."

"At least you stuck around, though. Hank is going to be kicking himself when he sees how well we're doing, once this lager gets released."

Cam rolled his eyes. "Hank is going to be sipping cocktails mixed by pool boys with pert little asses in the tropics for the next three years with his buy-out money. I doubt he'll regret getting out while he could anytime soon."

"Until the money runs out, at least. Seriously, Cam. I'm proud of you for sticking this out. Not everyone would have."

Cam raised his glass. "Wheelers don't back down, remember?"

I clinked my coffee cup against the pint. "Cheers to that, brother."

"Oh—don't they?" The door slammed behind Brendan as he stood there in a gust of snow flurries, a smug smile on his lips. "Hello, Royce."

Cam grunted, patting me on the shoulder and taking his leave. As I watched him leave, I couldn't help but envy him.

Instead, I finished my coffee and motioned for my pregnant ex to sit down at the table with me. "Hello, Brendan. Let's talk."

I didn't like the look he was giving me as he came toward me—and by the time he sat down, the smugness smeared all over his face had gotten even worse.

But Cam was right—Wheelers didn't back down.

***

The road to Patrick's house seemed longer than usual that night—not that it mattered. No amount of time could have prepared me for what I had to tell Patrick. I'd hoped by the end of the drive, I'd know what to say to him, but by the time I was knocking on his door, I still didn't even know how to say it.

"Royce." Patrick stood there in the doorway in his sweatpants and no shirt, rubbing his eyes. "Did you call? Sorry, I fell asleep…"

"Can I come in?" I asked, doing my best to block him the wind and snow. He looked so delicate and vulnerable, I didn't want him to catch cold.

"Yeah. Yeah, sure." Patrick moved aside and I slid past him into the hallway. "So … what's up?"

I immediately looked around for Thomas. Like many conversations I'd been having lately, this was one I would rather have without an audience.

"Don't worry. He's not here. We're alone." Patrick closed the door behind me and gave me a confused look. "Royce … why are you here? What's going on?"

I sighed, dragging my fingers through my hair. "I have something to tell you. Something I should have told you when he first showed up here in Carter's Crossing…"

"Brendan?"

I blinked several times, just processing it. "Yeah, actually. How did you know?"

Patrick laughed humorlessly. "Your pregnant ex-boyfriend doesn't just show up at your workplace for nothing. I was just waiting for you to tell me for yourself."

"Fuck. Patrick, I'm so sorry…"

Patrick crossed his arms over his perfectly chiseled bare chest. "So, is it yours?"

I blinked again. Obviously, I'd underestimated Patrick's powers of observation—and his ability to play things cool despite having figured this whole thing out weeks ago.

"Yeah," I finally said. "I didn't believe it at first, but apparently … he had the results of a paternity test with him when he showed up today. His baby is mine. It … it surprised the hell out of me, honestly. I didn't think…"

"But it is." Patrick nodded slowly. "I get it. That must have been a shock for you."

"It was," I admitted. "But … Patrick, I want you to know that this doesn't change how I feel about you."

"It changes some things, though," he said levelly.

"It … it does." I lowered my gaze. I'd expected Patrick to take this poorly— to yell at me, to throw things, to lose it over the realization that he wasn't the only man I'd gotten pregnant in the last few months.

But Patrick wasn't Brendan. Patrick was so much more, which made me feel even worse about what I had to tell him next.

"I take responsibility for my actions, Patrick. Whether or not I'm happy about the results. I told Brendan flat out that I had no intention of getting back together with him, but…"

"But you'll need to pay child support."

"Which means I'll need to go back to my job in New York. I'm not leaving you alone through this, either—and it's the only way I can support you both."

"Figured as much." Patrick went into the living room and sat on the sofa, resting his elbows on his knees and hunching over. "But there's no need. I'm good here, Royce. I don't need you to sacrifice anything just to keep me afloat."

"You don't need to do this alone."

"No, I don't." Patrick looked up at me with his clear green eyes. "But just because you're not here for me doesn't mean that I'll be alone. I've got people here, Royce. You don't have to worry about me."

"Don't I?"

He shook his head. "No, you don't."

"But … I want to be here for you, Patrick. If you want me to be, I mean."

He stared at the wall for a while before he looked back up at me again. "Honestly, Royce? Thank you for telling me. Really. But all things considered … I need a bit to think about this."

"That's … that's fair," I said. Even as I said it, though, it was breaking my heart. "I'll be in town for a couple of days still. If you come to any conclusions, I mean."

Patrick nodded. "Thanks. I'll let you know if I change my mind."

Seeing him like this, so put together and so calm, was almost worse than the yelling and screaming that Brendan had led me to expect. He was restraining himself with such elegance and poise, no matter how badly he was hurting on the inside.

I should have known Patrick better than this. He was stronger than I ever could have guessed. "Well … you have my number," I said softly.

"I have your number," Patrick echoed.

For a moment, I thought I ought to go to him. I thought that I should close the gap between us. Take him in my arms. Kiss him, and somehow prove to him that this didn't change anything about how I felt about him. How he must have known that I had always felt.

But it didn't feel right. As I looked down at him, I knew that it might not ever feel right again. With Brendan's revelation, everything really had changed between us. What had been a choice before—move to the city or let me stay in Carter's Crossing with him—had now become an ultimatum.

"I'm sorry," I told him simply.

"I know."

I moved to the door. "Have a good night, Patrick."

He didn't even look over his shoulder at me as I went. "Have a good night, Royce."

Chapter 16

Patrick

"Headed to work?"

I looked back as Tom wandered out of his room, messy-haired and yawning. It was one of the benefits of being a wedding planner, I supposed. Tom only worked brunch hours and weekends, and spent the rest of the time sleeping in.

I held my keys up and jingled them for him. "Just heading in for the lunch rush. I'll be back for dinner."

"Not going out with Royce tonight?" Tom popped the fridge open and scanned it for provisions. "He can't be in town for much longer—figured you'd want to say goodbye."

I lowered the keys and looked away. Things hadn't really been the same between Royce and me since he'd told me about Brendan, and it was obvious why. Royce was headed back into the city, and I still wasn't sold on leaving Carter's Crossing—especially not for good. I hadn't even told my dad about the pregnancy yet, let alone faced him with the possibility that I could be moving to New York.

"If I see him, I see him," I said with a sigh. "He's got his own shit going on right now."

Tom grabbed a carton of leftover General Tsos' from the fridge and closed the door with an identical sigh. "You know that you're not in this alone, right? Whatever's going on between you and Royce, I'm still here for you."

"I know." I forced a smile. "Thanks, Tom."

"Go get 'em, Pat."

At the diner, the lunch rush went like it always did. The Petersons ordered burgers, the Joneses ordered the fish, the cook had to be reminded not to overcook the steaks, and by the time it was over, everyone was more than ready to go home. Dad and I spent the last hours of the afternoon working the books and writing paychecks. All the while, I was looking for the right moment to tell him—and all the while, I was failing to find it.

Finally, as we were packing up to leave, I knew that if I didn't bite the bullet and do it then, I wouldn't get up the courage to tell him again. And as much as I enjoyed the idea of playing off my baby bump as the result of overindulging in the Lonely Heart's pie selection, when I went into labor, that story would reach the end of its line.

"Dad…" I said softly as he cashed out the register. "I need to tell you something, and I want to know you don't have to worry."

Dad looked up from the till with concern written all over his face. "Funny, Pat—the way you phrased that is exactly the kind of thing that makes me worry."

I sat down at one of the bar stool on the other side of the counter and tried to give him a reassuring look. "It's just … before I tell you, I need you to understand that I've thought this through. I'm going to be able to be responsible about it—and I promise, I'm not going to let you down."

Suddenly, Dad's look of concern turned to a wide grin. "Pat … I knew we'd been working toward this anyway, so I can't say I'm surprised, but I *am* impressed. I've been waiting for this moment for a long time now, and I have to say, son, I'm just … I'm just so proud of you."

What? Whatever I was expecting to hear from him, that sure as hell wasn't it. "Dad … what do you think I'm trying to tell you?" I asked, raising an eyebrow.

"Well, that you're ready to take over the diner now, of course!"

Maybe it was the hormones, or maybe it was just so ridiculous that there was nothing else to do. The laughter bubbled up from deep within me and fell from my lips, filling the diner with its sound.

"That's not … *quite* what I wanted to say, Dad," I finally managed to get out when I regained enough composure to speak again. "I'm not taking over the diner just yet. I'm pregnant."

Dad's jaw dropped. He closed the cash register with a gentle *ding!* and stared at me for several long moments before he was able to react further.

"Well … I suppose that makes sense too, then," he said, shaking his head and letting out a little laugh of his own. He reached for a rag, busying his hands with wiping down the counter while his brain processed the big news. "Who's the alpha? That Wheeler boy you've been seeing lately?"

I nodded. "Royce—not Cam."

"He going to help support you? I don't want to force a shotgun wedding if I don't have to, but…"

"He's offered," I said with a laugh. "The real question is whether or not I'm going to let him."

"Why wouldn't you? Patrick … it's not easy raising a child alone. I know that better than just about anyone. Don't you want to give your baby more than I was able to give you?"

"You gave me plenty, Dad." I sighed. "It's … it's complicated. I mean, it would have been complicated no matter what—Royce belongs in New York, and I belong here."

"Not necessarily." Dad held my gaze as he wiped his hands on his apron and laid one atop mine. "You want to go to the city and start your family, Pat, I'm not gonna stop you."

"But the diner…"

"You know why I care so much about this diner, Pat—and not meaning to offend, but it's got nothing to do with you. This place is the last thing I've got of your alpha dad, is all. But if letting it go means that you and your alpha and your baby can have a real family … well, maybe letting go could be good for all of us."

It was so strange hearing those words come out of his mouth, I didn't know what to say. These last few months I'd been so worried about hurting Dad's feelings about the diner that I'd never even considered asking him if there wasn't some other path for me. But now that he was proposing it himself, I didn't know that I even wanted what he was offering.

"It's more complicated than me staying or going, though. Royce … I'm not the only pregnant omega in his life right now."

"He's got *another* baby on the way?" If my previous revelations weren't enough to knock Dad off his feet, that one just about did it. "Pat, what kind of man is this Royce of yours anyway?"

I shook my head, sensing his concern. "I know how it seems, Dad, but Royce didn't do it intentionally. At least, I don't think he did. As soon as I found out I was pregnant, this other omega showed up with a wild story and a baby bump."

"And Royce is sure this other baby is his?"

"Paternity test says it is."

Dad pursed his lips until they created a thin, white line. "You sure you don't want me to go grab the shotgun?"

"Not necessary, Dad. Royce has made his choices already. Now I need to make mine."

My dad sighed, then pulled out a leftover pie from the lunch service and cut us each a slice. He slid mine toward me with a fork, sending the smell of apples, cinnamon, and brown sugar wafting through the air.

"Did I ever tell you the story of Thomas and Michael Carter?" He topped the pie with whipped cream and nodded at me. "Go on. Eat it. You need enough pie for two now."

"We learned about them in school, I think. Different story every year. It never sounded like anyone really knew which tale was the real one." I dug into the pie with my fork, not feeling much of an appetite, but not dumb enough to refuse. If I'd learned anything growing up being raised by my omega dad, it was that pie had healing properties—and even if it didn't, it was good enough that it didn't matter.

"The founders of our little town here are hard to pin down when it comes to their real backstory." Dad leveled a mouthful of his own pie toward his lips. "Some say they were two soldiers on different sides of the Civil War who came together, wounded and in need. Others say Thomas was lost here in the mountains and Michael found him, blue with cold and freezing to death."

"Nursed him back to health and was pregnant with his child come spring. I remember."

"Some of the stories are more unlikely than others, of course. I don't know about you, but I've never met anyone who really believed that Thomas was, for example, a human cursed to take the shape of a bear, and that Michael's love was the only thing that could set him free."

"I don't know about that. I've seen the mural of them over at the community center. Don't know who the artist was—but Thomas sure looked like a bear to me."

Dad laughed, flicking whipped cream at me. "Your alpha dad told me the same thing once. You know why the stories are so ridiculous, though, right?"

"Makes for better mural paintings than the truth?"

Dad shook his head. "No matter who Thomas and Michael were, the moral of their story is the same. No matter what happens, love finds a way. No matter the hurdles. No matter the setbacks. Love conquers all in the end."

I stared hard at the pie. "That's sweet, Dad. But this isn't a fairy tale—it's my real life."

"Oh, come on." Dad flipped through his phone and quickly pulled up a picture. "Are you really going to tell this little guy he doesn't get his happily ever after?"

I looked up at the picture and saw my own face grinning back at me. I couldn't have been more than two or three in it. Dad was younger by a couple decades as he bounced me on his knee. And there behind us was my alpha dad, green-eyed and bearded, looking an awful lot like a bear himself. He gave off that vibe that he'd do anything he could to protect my omega dad and me. In the end, I guessed in a way, he had.

"Whatever happens, it'll be okay," my omega dad reassured me. "If I can give you any advice, Patrick, it's this—if you really care about Royce, don't let him go. You never know how long you'll have him for, but you'll always be glad for the time you shared."

It made my heart ache just thinking about it. My omega dad had only been with my alpha dad for five short years before we'd lost him, but he'd mourned him for every year since. And in just these few months with Royce, I'd finally been able to feel a glimmer of that kind of connection.

The promise of it made my decision that much harder. There was so much about Royce that had been giving me reservations, but at the same time, there was so much about him that I wanted to learn. Wanted to experience and enjoy and know.

"Drive home safe, son." Dad gathered up the pie plates and waved off my attempts to help him wash up. "And remember to honk before Devil's Bend. You've got my grandchild in the car with you now."

"Love you, Dad," I told him.

He grinned at me, then disappeared into the diner's kitchen. "Love you too, Pat. Love you both."

The whole ride home, I contemplated how things must have been for my omega dad after my alpha dad's passing. Being a single father wouldn't be any walk in the park … but he'd done it, hadn't he? Despite all the challenges he'd faced, I'd turned out okay—apart from getting pregnant out of wedlock and branding myself as the town harlot.

On the other hand, the loss of my alpha dad had always been present in my childhood. Family dinners that should have been rich and full of life had sometimes ended in mournful tears. That wasn't the life I'd ever imagined for my own child … but if things with Royce didn't work out, I might not have a choice.

After all the brooding and debating I'd been doing, I'd figured that at least some of it would've resolved something. But as it turned out, it hadn't gotten me anywhere but home.

In times like this, there was nothing left to do but distract myself. I pulled out the old sketch that I'd started the day I met Royce—the one with two men walking through the woods—and lost myself in the lines and shadows of their forms.

By the time I was done for the night, I'd smudged and scribbled the sketch so much that it was difficult to tell if there were two figures at all anymore, or if there was only one.

Chapter 17

Royce

I hefted the last of my suitcases up out of the gravel and into the trunk of my car. Standing there staring at the only belongings I'd needed for the last two months made going back to all my possessions and city luxuries seem a little silly. If I only needed two suitcases of clothing, my phone, my wallet, and my keys to survive, why the hell did I have an entire apartment full over overpriced things?

Carter's Crossing had rubbed off on me, I guessed. Life was simpler up here in the mountains. I'd simplified mine to match.

In that regard, I wasn't looking forward to heading back to New York at all. Things were so damn complex there—and the drama with Brendan was only half of it. Answering to my clients about where I'd disappeared to for two months without warning was going to take more energy than I wanted to expend, and then there was the issue of my boss…

But my reservations about going back to the city ran deeper than all that. Leaving Carter's Crossing meant leaving more than just the brewery, the mountains, and my memories here behind.

When I heard the gravel crunch behind me, my heart leaped in my chest. The hardest thing of all to leave behind was going to be Patrick, and I'd been holding out hope that maybe, somehow, he'd find some way to forgive me for everything, at least enough to come and see me before I left. To say goodbye.

But when I turned, I was only met with Brendan's smug smirk. "Going back home now, huh?" He placed a hand on his hip and eyed my suitcases filling up the trunk.

"Looks like," I grunted. I was being as polite as I could to Brendan—especially now that I'd been enough of an asshole to doubt his claims of carrying my child—but with his attitude, and the slimy way he'd been trying to weasel his way back into my life, it was hard not to resent him a little.

"And you're ready to attend to your responsibilities? Because—just in case I didn't make this clear earlier—there *will* be responsibilities, Royce."

I nodded, reaching into my wallet and pulling out a card. "Get into contact with Ryan when you're back in the city. He'll help you sort out what you'll need from me."

When I handed the card to Brendan, he pulled a face. "This is your lawyer's card, Royce."

"Looks like," I said again.

"You're seriously going to field all my needs through your fucking *lawyer*?"

"He'll make sure you get what you want. Money. Baby supplies." I sighed. "My time. You're just going to have to go through him to get it. Once we have a contract ironed out, I'll do whatever I have to."

"What if the things I need aren't … *appropriate* for contract law?" Brendan moved toward me coyly, popping up on his tiptoes and aiming a kiss at my lips.

I pressed my palm against his chest and held him back as I closed the trunk. "Not happening, Brendan. We're not getting back together. You can have whatever you want from me—but not that."

Brendan deflated, taking a few steps back. "Yeah, yeah. I know. I'm just so fucking horny, Royce."

He posed, running his hands over his swelling stomach in a way that I'm sure some alphas would have found attractive—just not me. "All these baby hormones have me wanting sex, like, all the fucking time."

For a moment, I wondered if Patrick might be feeling the same way. If it had been Patrick standing there, showing off his baby bump for me and begging for a kiss, he would have had it and then some.

"See you in the city, Royce." Brendan's pout turned into an exasperated eye roll. "Tell your lawyer to expect me."

Even after Brendan had gone, the thought of a horny, hormone-crazed, pregnant Patrick was still on my mind. He'd been on my mind almost constantly since the last time I'd seen him, in every iteration of himself my brain could conjure.

At breakfast, I imagined Patrick wearing a cute little apron and eating pancakes off of my fork. In the afternoons, I imagined him in a coat and gloves, building snowmen with a dark-haired toddler in the tentative winter sun. And at night…

At night, I imagined him in every position possible, though the only one that would've really mattered was the one where he was in bed next to me, right there by my side.

I thought about calling him. My thumb hovered over Patrick's name in my phone for longer than I wanted to admit.

But if Patrick had wanted to talk to me before I left, he'd known where to find me. The fact that he hadn't come around to see me off told me everything I needed to know about how he felt about me—and it didn't matter how the hell I felt in return.

Instead, I dialed my boss up. I'd been dreading talking to Don ever since I'd caught him fucking Brendan in the boardroom, and with good reason. What the fuck was I supposed to say to him? *Hey, Don. Headed back to work tomorrow, so if you have any kinky office liaisons planned, maybe lock the door this time?*

But as it turned out, talking to Don ended up being even weirder than I could have imagined.

"Royce! Hell, it's good to hear your voice again." I could hear the thrumming of house bass in the background as Don yelled over the cheering of a crowd. "Fuck me, didn't think I'd be getting a call from you again! You ready to come back to work?"

I shook my head at Don being out at a club right now—especially in the middle of the damn day. He was a few years older than I was, but where I'd long since left the party-boy life behind me, he was obviously more reluctant to give his playboy lifestyle up.

"S'pose I am," I grunted. It felt all too much like I was coming back to the city with my tail between my legs at this point, but I'd made my bed. Just because it was in the doghouse didn't mean I wasn't going to lie in it. "How've things been without me?"

Don groaned. The fading noises of the crowd told me he was deigning to take a step away from grinding on glittered-up omegas in tight pants long enough to talk to me. "Christ, Royce. You've got no idea. The clients haven't liked a single thing that Richards has whipped up for them…"

I couldn't help but chuckle at that. "We've gotta work on Richards. He's still resistant to the thought of making his ideas seem like they were the client's ideas all along."

"That's what I've been saying. Fuck, we've missed you! Between Richards shitting the bed left and right for two months straight, and the mess that your slutty little omega made of the office…"

"Wait, what?" I blinked, briefly considering that I might have heard Don wrong. "Brendan wrecked the office?"

"Oh, more than wrecked it. Chucked my desk chair out the window, for one—and from the twenty-third story, mind you, so our insurance rates are through the damn *roof* now—"

"Why did Brendan do that?" Not that Brendan ever needed an excuse for drama—but a desk chair out the window was a lot, even for him.

"Hell if I know. I chalked it up to pregnancy hormones—you know how these omegas get. That's how it is for men like us, Royce. When they come sniffing around, pretending that they've got their eyes on your ass, when really, they're just trying to size up your wallet …

"Don't worry, though," he reassured me. "No bad blood between us, Royce. If I'd have known all the trouble fucking your man was going to get me into, I would have saved myself the child support checks and kept my dick in my pants. Guess I did us both a favor, huh?"

Child support? That didn't check out. There was only one reason that Don would be writing child support checks for Brendan—and it was the same reason I was returning to my job with Don in the city to begin with.

"Don … spell this out for me. You're saying *you're* the one who got Brendan pregnant?"

"Ugh. Just my luck, right?" Don laughed dryly. "Didn't believe it myself—so I dragged him down to the clinic and had him get a paternity test to be sure. Not before he'd already thrown my desk out the window, of course. It's gonna be hell on my paycheck, but what can you do? Medical science doesn't lie."

Don had a point—or at least, he would have, if Brendan hadn't also presented me with the same fucking story. The only difference was that Don had taken Brendan to get the test done himself, whereas I'd only seen a set of results from god knew where.

"I've gotta go, Don. Enjoy your party."

"Damn right I will! If I'm going to be changing diapers in a few months, you bet your ass I'm going to enjoy myself while I still can. See you on Monday?"

I didn't answer. I wasn't sure what to say. Besides, the clinic in town would be closing in under half an hour—and I needed to get there before I ran out of time.

"I'm here to check up on some paternity results," I told the woman behind the counter at the clinic.

She huffed with annoyance—which was probably warranted. I'd only come through the doors with five minutes to spare before closing time. But when she looked up at me through her horn-rimmed glasses, she didn't seem impatient.

"I don't know how many times I have to tell you crazy alphas," she said with an eye-roll. "We don't *do* those here. You want to find out if the baby is yours or not, head into the city or consider monogamy."

And there it was. Everything that Brendan had told me had been a lie. Hell, if it wasn't for the way he'd been flaunting his baby bump, I would have assumed that he'd been faking that too. But while Brendan might have been pregnant, Don's story, and the lack of a paternity test at the Carter's Crossing clinic, told me everything I needed to know.

Whoever the father of Brendan's child was, it sure as hell wasn't me.

The revelation cut deep, like an incision made to draw out a splinter buried beneath the skin. Now that it was over, there was a sense of relief. Whatever went on with Brendan, his child and his life now had nothing to do with me.

But the fact that I'd nearly lost Patrick over Brendan's lie—the fact that I'd nearly had the life I'd always worried was too good for me to want, only for Brendan to come out of the woodwork and try to snatch it away—that was a wound that was going to fester.

And dammit, I wasn't going to let it.

"Don?" I called him from the road, remembering just in time to honk my horn as I took the curve of Devil's Bend.

"Royce! Are you back in the city yet?" Don sounded like he'd had a shot of rum or four since we'd last talked. "You've gotta get down to the Peel *stat*, Royce. They've got these new dancers here that you're gonna *love*. Blue eyes, blonde hair, and the tightest little—"

"Don." I paused, making sure he was listening to me.

"Yeah, Royce?"

"Don, consider this my notice. It looks like I'm not coming back to the city after all."

"What? Why?"

Despite myself, when I checked my rear view mirror, I realized I was smiling. "Got some unfinished business to settle up. Tell Richards to stop treating his proposals like he's selling used cars, okay? He'll clean up just fine."

"You're serious about this? Shit!" Don swore away from the phone for a few seconds, like I couldn't make out every single word he was spitting. "But Royce, buddy! New York is your playground! Your kingdom, your home!"

"I've got a new home now. Best of luck, Don. And lay off the drink, okay? You've got a baby to think of now."

My smile widened as I hung up the phone and pulled into the driveway of the diner. There was only one car left out in the parking lot, and I knew whose it was.

I should have done this a long time ago—but I would fix that little lapse in judgment tonight.

Chapter 18

Patrick

That morning, I woke up feeling worse than ever. There was at least one good reason why: I'd fallen asleep sketching at my desk, which meant my back was killing me. But even after having a hot shower and scrubbing the charcoal off my cheek, I wasn't feeling entirely up to speed.

Unfortunately, for the first time in as long as I could remember, Dad wasn't picking up his phone.

"Hey, Dad. Feeling a little under the weather this morning," I informed his voice mail instead. "I was hoping that you'd be able to open the diner without me this morning. Call back and let me know?"

I shuffled around the kitchen for a while, brewing a cup of the green tea that I was replacing my morning coffee with. I even made some whole grain toast, so I didn't have to take the prenatal vitamins I'd picked up at the pharmacy on an empty stomach.

None of it seemed to have any effect, though. I was in a slump, and it was more than just a lack of self-care or a bad night's sleep. My future felt more up in the air than it ever had before, and to a certain extent, there was nothing I could do about it.

Royce was leaving today, and we still hadn't resolved anything between us. I'd been hoping maybe he'd call or something, but my phone was silent as ever. If I was waiting some kind of ridiculous grand gesture—a baby buggy full of roses or, better yet, proof that Brendan was having John Stamos' baby instead—I knew better than to hold my breath.

I missed Royce. I wanted Royce. But no matter what my dad said about Carter's Crossing finding a way to bring people together, I knew exactly how this story ended.

Royce would go back to the city, and I'd be left here to face fatherhood on my own. It wasn't the happy ending that romance novels had promised me, but that was real life for you.

With another call to Dad sent to his voicemail, I washed up the breakfast dishes and walked to Tom's bedroom door. Happy ending or no, there was no way

I was going to be up for going into the diner today. If I didn't know for sure that

Dad could open on his own, I'd have to find someone to cover for me.

Tom tended to flirt more with the customers than he served them, but he'd

usually made out okay in tips when he'd covered for me before. I figured I'd see if

he'd head in to open the diner in my place—but when I knocked on the door, I

didn't even hear one of Thomas' patented early-morning fuck-you groans.

"Where the hell *is* everyone today?" I grumbled as I headed out to my truck.

So much for everyone being here for me through this pregnancy—if I couldn't

even trust them to be able to cover a shift for me, how did they expect me to trust

them to get me to the hospital when I went into labor?

I'd end up having Royce's baby in my own bathtub at this rate.

As I neared Devil's Bend, my head was too full of worry and frustration to

be able to concentrate on the road. But for Devil's Bend, I always managed to draw

myself out of my own whining long enough to take the turn nice and slow.

It was a good thing, too. Just as I was raising my hand to the horn to give the

oncoming traffic a courtesy honk, another vehicle tore around the curve, veering

wildly into my lane. I was only just barely able to hit my brakes and slide over in

time to avoid a head-on collision—but when the car had passed and I was able to ease my truck into a forward motion again, it wasn't the near-wreck that had my heart pounding.

It was the face of the driver who'd nearly hit me that was making my breath go short. Unless I was hallucinating—and I doubted that was the case—it had been Royce's ex, Brendan, behind the wheel of that car. He'd looked absolutely furious, and his driving had reflected that.

Arrogant prick. He was getting everything—the baby, the big-city life, and more likely than not, the man I'd almost let myself fall in love with as a cherry on top. What the hell did he have to be so pissed off about?

It wasn't until I got to the diner that it hit me that maybe Brendan wasn't getting everything he'd wanted after all. I didn't want to let myself start to hope, but once the seed was planted, it was hard to make it stop taking root.

Could Royce have changed his mind about leaving? It seemed too good to be true, but it would have explained Brendan's behavior.

My hopes only rose higher as I turned my key in the lock of the diner's back door—and realized it wasn't necessary. The door was already open, and as soon as I walked through it, a flurry of delicious smells hit me, just like Brendan's car almost had.

Buttercream. Champagne. Roses—and, if I was smelling things right, a fresh batch of my omega dad's boysenberry pie. It had been my alpha dad's favorite, which meant we only made it for special occasions.

My omega dad liked Saturdays as much as the next guy—but not even the best day of the weekend would normally have called for a boysenberry pie.

I moved past the kitchen with hesitation, still trying to guess at what the hell was going on here. There was a clamor of noise, contained behind the door to the kitchen, that I normally would have wanted to check out—no one should have been there other than my dad that morning, but it sounded like there was a full crew manning the grill already.

As I moved deeper into the diner, I found rose petals beneath my feet. They seemed to be leading out to the main seating area … and where rose petals led, I followed.

But no amount of flowers and tantalizing scents could have prepared me for what I found when I walked through the diner's staff door.

He was even handsomer than he'd been when I'd first met him—and that was saying something. His dark hair was slicked back elegantly in that classic

Clark Kent style. His shoulders cut a wide figure beneath the fabric of a black designer tux.

His amber eyes captured my greens with his gaze immediately. "Patrick. I—" Royce paused, looking me up and down. "Wow. You look incredible."

I looked down at what I was wearing—nothing special, believe me. Jeans. A t-shirt—not even a *nice* t-shirt.

"You clean up pretty well yourself." I could hear the trepidation in my own voice. Part of me knew what had to be happening right now—but the other part of me was still too wrapped up in doubt to believe it. "Royce, what's all this about?"

"You, Patrick." Royce grinned. "It's all about you."

"I'm…" *Flattered? Excited? Scared?* "I'm listening."

"Patrick, I…" Royce hung his head for a moment, and gave an embarrassed laugh. "Would you believe that I had a whole speech planned out for this? You'd think you were one of my marketing clients, the way I had this thing prepped."

"I can believe it." I nodded, trying not to appear over-eager, but the truth was that my breaths were coming in short and sharp, and I could hear my heart beating in my ears. "I'd like to hear it, actually. Unless you've forgotten?"

Royce shook his head. "I never forget a good speech. It went something like: 'Patrick Murray, you are the love of my life. Not just because I fell for you, but because you taught me how to love in the first place.'"

His eyes sparkled as he gave a self-deprecating little laugh. "Then I thought I'd wax poetic about the meaning of love for a little while. Give a little color to the presentation, you know."

"I can imagine," I told him, nodding again. "Go on."

"Then I thought I'd talk about the cynical, stuck-up bastard I was before I met you." He took a step closer to me, slowly, like he was afraid any too-sudden movement might cause me to bolt. "How you gave me faith in something I never even believed in."

"Poetic." My voice was barely a whisper now. Royce was just close enough to hear it. "And then?"

Royce reached beneath his jacket and produced a little champagne-colored velvet box as he dropped to one knee. "And then I'd say, 'Patrick Murray, will you marry me?'"

I had to do it. I reached over, felt my left bicep, and found enough purchase in the muscle there so I could pinch myself.

I had to be dreaming. There was no other option. This was something straight from the script of one of my weird, fantastical pregnancy dreams. There was no way that this was happening in real life.

But I didn't wake up at the pinch. I felt it, as honest and visceral as anything else I'd been feeling since Royce had come swaggering into my life. No matter how hard I blinked, concentrated or double-taked, Royce didn't go away.

Out of the corner of my eye, I even saw my father and Thomas appear— which was how I knew that it had to be real. I'd dealt with Tom's shit too much while I was awake for my subconscious to ever inject him into my dreams.

"Trust me, Sleeping Beauty," Royce quipped with a smirk. "You're not dreaming. Should I ask you again, or…?"

"Yes." The word left my lips half a second before I threw my arms around Royce's neck, sending both of us tumbling to the ground. My lips found his, tasting mint and boysenberries.

I only pulled away so I could tell him yes again.

In the moments after, Royce told me everything. All of it. His call with Don. Figuring out Brendan's lie. With some pressing, Royce even produced the paternity test that Brendan had photoshopped to back up his claim that Royce was his baby's father, with Tom jumping in to show me exactly how he knew it'd been doctored.

"Okay, okay." I held my hands up and took a deep breath. "Then … all of this?"

I gestured to the diner space, which had been transformed by some kind of matrimonial magic into the venue of an absolute dream wedding.

"That was me," Tom admitted with a sheepish grin. "Honestly, I'm hurt that you didn't recognize my handiwork."

"Royce drove over just as I was opening the place up for the day," my dad explained. "Asked me for my permission and everything. *I'm* hurt that you didn't introduce me to him earlier—but he's rectified that now."

Dad's eyes were glistening with pride. "You've caught yourself a hell of a man, Pat. Reminds me of your alpha dad a little, even."

For the first time ever, I noticed the slightest tinge of pink around Royce's ears. It didn't stop him from drawing the ring he'd bought me out of its box and slipping it onto my finger. The band glistened, silver and perfect, in the twinkling lights that Tom had strung overhead.

"Say it again," Royce commanded me. "Tell me you're going to be my husband."

"Yes," I blurted out immediately. "Yes—god, absolutely. Yes, Royce." I was grinning so hard, my face hurt. "I'm going to marry you, Royce. I'll be yours if you'll be mine."

"Good," Tom said, catching me under the arm and dragging me away from Royce as I moved in to seal the proposal with another kiss.

"Hey! What the hell—"

"You can kiss your Prince Charming later." Tom hauled me back through the staff door and into my office, only giving Royce time to give me a gentle wave goodbye. "We're doing this wedding *now*."

"But I don't have anything to—"

"Wear?" Tom reached behind my office door, smirking impishly as he produced a pristine white tux. "I didn't go through all this trouble for nothing, dummy. Yes means yes—we're doing this now."

"Here?" The word came out on the end of a laugh. This was all happening so fast—not that I minded. Every bad feeling in my bones had been washed away with Royce's revelation. Now I was just trying to catch my breath.

"We would have had it out at the family barn," Tom explained, sighing wistfully at the thought of how beautiful the trees in the orchard would have looked glistening with twinkle lights and dusted with fresh-fallen snow. "But those greedy Taggart bastards…"

"Lawsuit. Right." I ran my tongue over my lips as I glanced at my tux—the tux I'd be wearing when I said my vows to Royce. "But are you sure…?"

"What's there left to be *un*sure about, Pat? The city boy loves you. You love him. You're having his baby, and he wants to make you his husband. Get with the program—we're already off-schedule here." Tom eyed me up and down critically, bristling with his infectious wedding-planner energy. "Unless you'd rather get married in your Converse and jeans?"

"No," I said with a laugh. "Pass me the tux. Let's do this thing."

Chapter 19

Royce

On a Saturday, in the Lonely Hearts diner, I married the love of my life. His father cried; Nicky sobbed on the shoulder of the burly biker he'd introduced us to as his new boyfriend; and even Tom turned away briefly during the vows, dabbling at his nose with his handkerchief and muttering about having *something in his eye*.

"I love you, Patrick," I told my new husband for the first time as I slid a ring onto his finger. "Rich, poor—in sickness, in health—whatever happens. Whatever it takes. I love you. I'm yours."

"You'd better be," Patrick choked out on the end of a ragged laugh. Even when he was trying not to tear up, he was the most exquisite thing I'd ever seen. "I love you too, Royce. I love you in this moment right now. I'll love you twenty years from now. I'll love you forever—and I'll love you beyond that, too."

When we kissed, it was just as passionate as our first time. Patrick's dad and I might have talked Tom out of setting off fireworks indoors at such a short notice, but when Patrick's lips met mine, a light show of color exploded behind my eyes.

He tasted like green tea and fresh jam when we kissed at the altar—but by the end of the night, he tasted like buttercream icing and boysenberry pie.

"God," Cam moaned as he slipped another forkful of our wedding pie between his lips. "Get married every week from here on out, okay? I'd kill for more of this pie."

"Ask Patrick's dad for the recipe." I elbowed him in the ribs as Cam eyed the dwindling pie resources at the buffet with regret. "You're gonna pop your tuxedo if you eat another slice. Some best man you are."

Cam laughed. "That'll be one for the wedding album. You and Patrick ready to head out?"

I glanced over at Patrick, who was doubled over in laughter at something that Tom had said. He looked so damn good in his tux, it would be a shame to get him out of it ... but somehow, I knew that I'd enjoy the look of those pants on the floor even more than I liked them around his hips.

"I've been ready to get him out of here since the *I dos*," I admitted. "But he seems to be having such a good time…"

Cam groaned good-naturedly. "If you would have told me two months ago that I'd be running interference so my brother could get a chance to make sweet love to my ex…"

"Careful," I warned him, grinning. "That's my husband you're talking about."

"I'm proud of you, man." Cam clapped me on the shoulder and headed over to distract Tom. I followed him, ready to whisk Patrick away at the first chance I got. "Hell, maybe even I'll jump on the wedding bandwagon soon."

"You? Married?" I considered giving him more shit about the audacity of that idea, but then thought better of it. "You never know. Might suit you."

"Hey," Patrick yawned as I slipped into place at his side. Right where I belonged.

"Hey. Wanna get out of here?"

Patrick narrowed his eyes, kittenish. "To what end, husband?"

"The happy kind." I pulled him into a kiss as I tugged him toward the door. "The happiest ending I can give you, I hope."

"Promises, promises," Patrick cooed, settling comfortably beneath my arm.

And when I got him back to his place, I made good on every one of them.

"God," Patrick gasped as I tore his boxers down with my teeth. The rest of our clothes left a trail from the front door all the way to the bed. "You're hungry tonight—didn't you eat at the reception?"

"Different kind of hunger," I growled, lapping at the rippled V of his pelvis. "The kind only you can satisfy."

I flipped him over, balancing the roughness that my cock was demanding with the gentleness that Patrick's body required. I caressed his belly with one hand, cradling it softly with my palm, while I spread his ass with the other, kissing the hardness of his curves.

"Fuck," Patrick whimpered. "Royce … lick me."

Eager to please, I slipped my tongue between his ass cheeks and rimmed his tight, hot hole. He tasted different now that he was pregnant—slicker and sweeter, like honey. It was addictive, but not so addictive that I could ignore how hard he was making my cock.

"Fuck me," Patrick begged. "Please, Royce—take me."

I smoothed my hands down over his shoulders and positioned myself against him. Patrick wasn't a simpering virgin anymore—he was a hot, wet, desperate omega now, fearlessly swimming in desire and pregnant with my child.

"I love you." My cock slipped inside him, stretching him to fit the thickness of my shaft perfectly. "I love you, Patrick Wheeler. I love you."

"I love you," he moaned back. "Fuck—I love you, Royce. I love you!"

Our bodies moved together, driven with need. His muscles tensed and relaxed with pleasure as I fed him inch after inch of my cock. Before long, he was bucking his hips back to sink me deeper. I met his movements with even harder thrusts. I wanted to be balls deep in Patrick—balls deep in my husband. In the omega who would give birth to my child.

"Fuck, Royce. I'm close—I'm so close!"

"Give it to me, then." I laid my body over his, scraping my teeth against his neck. "Come for me, Patrick. I want it—I want you. I love you. Come for me!"

"Yes!" Patrick let out an animalistic cry as his ass spasmed around my cock. "God, yes, Royce! I love you! I fucking love you!"

"Take it, Patrick! Take my cum!" My balls tensed against him, flooding him with my cum. It rushed out of my cock so quickly and with so much force, I was dizzied by the raw pleasure of it all.

I laid back after I withdrew from him, but Patrick wasn't satisfied yet.

"Let me lick you." He hovered over the tip of my cock with his mouth. "Let me suck you clean."

I took my cock at the base and pressed it between his wet, warm lips. Patrick sucked cock like he did anything else—with passion. With focus.

With love.

If I hadn't just emptied everything my balls had into his ass, he would have made me come again.

"You're mine," I purred, pulling him up to rest his cheek on my chest. My arm curled around him protectively as his body rubbed against mine. "You belong to me, Patrick Wheeler."

I felt him smile against my pec. "Patrick Wheeler …I could get used to that name. I'm yours now." He nodded slightly, yawning and stretching. His body felt completely relaxed against mine. Completely at home. "I'll always be yours."

"God … I'm going to be a dad." He felt so right at my side, I couldn't help but bask in the sheer fucking joy he made me feel. "You're going to give me a baby."

"Is that what you want, Royce?"

I laughed. "I married you, Patrick. I don't take that lightly. There were times that I never thought I would find this … but now, I know that I was just waiting for you. For us. For our family."

My fingertips brushed over his stomach. It was still so flat, gorgeous abs and warm skin, but soon I knew it would grow big and round as our baby grew inside him. "I want to be a dad just as much as I want to be your husband."

"Well, you've got us," Patrick assured me. "You're completely right—we're yours."

He fell asleep on my chest not long after, mumbling sleepily about his plans for our future. We knew that we were going to stay in Carter's Crossing, but beyond that, the future was whatever we wanted it to be.

I was too excited to sleep just then, though. I found myself picking up our abandoned clothes and searching around for hangers for our tuxes in the dark. I didn't dare risk turning on the overhead lights and waking Patrick, but I thought the lamp at his desk might be enough to see by.

I just wasn't prepared for what I would find when I flipped on that desk light.

"What are you over there gasping over?" Patrick asked sleepily, rolling over and rubbing his eyes.

I picked the sketch up gingerly at the corners, careful not to smudge any of it. "Your art, Patrick. Wow … why didn't you tell me you were so talented?"

Patrick squinted at the swirling colors and shades of the piece I'd found at his desk. It was two men, their bodies in silhouette among the trees. They walked hand in hand toward a kaleidoscopic sunset, looking certain of each other and completely in love.

"It's nothing." Patrick waved the compliment away. "Stop fawning over my sketching and come to bed."

"Pat, this belongs in a gallery. You should be getting paid for this."

"It's *nothing*," he insisted again. "I'm not ready to go pro yet. This is just … I dunno. A labor of love."

I stared at him for a long moment, watching the way his body looked in the low light with the sheets tangled about him just so. He wasn't just an artist—he was a work of art. He was mine.

And to my surprise … he'd just given me an idea.

"Patrick, you're a genius." I kissed him deeply as I slipped back into bed with him, leaving the sketch on the desk where I'd found it. "You're absolutely *brilliant*, you gorgeous, perfect thing!"

"I am?" Patrick laughed as I laid down a dozen kisses on his neck and chest. "How?"

"I'll tell you in the morning," I said with a yawn. My eyes were finally getting heavy, and my heart was full of warmth. With Patrick in my arms, I knew I could do anything—but I would do it in the damn morning, after I'd finished taking my time with my husband. With my family. "Tonight, let's just be together."

"Whatever you say, handsome," Patrick purred. Then his fingers brushed against my cock, stirring it back to life in an instant. "Want to go again before bed?"

If I was sleepy before that question, I was anything but after it.

"Oh, absolutely." I moved over him, settling my hips between his thighs and my hard, throbbing cock against his. "Thought you'd never ask."

Chapter 20

Patrick

Cam laid the money down on the bar, and a cheer rang out through the air. "That's ninety-nine thousand, nine hundred and ninety-nine." Cam glanced at Royce. "You ready to do this?"

But Royce hesitated, giving me a last-minute concerned look. "Pat, if you don't want me to—"

"No," I said with a laugh. My hands were resting on my pregnant belly, cradling it gently. "Have the beer, Royce. My man has earned it."

Royce echoed my laugh as he dipped down to kiss me, then slapped the money down on the bar. Another cheer rang out as Nicky pulled out two frosty bottles of Cam's special beer—A Lager of Love, they were calling it. When I saw my art on the label, I couldn't help but beam with pride.

Royce had insisted on using my piece with the two lovers holding hands at sunset for the beer's label and promotional materials. It was my first commission as a real artist—but not my last. Cam and Royce had already commissioned me for new pieces to use for an IPA, a white blonde and a wheat beer, and knowing them, they had even bigger plans for expansion in the future.

Nicky popped the tops of both beers and handed them off to Cam and Royce. "And that makes one hundred thousand bottles of Lager of Love sold to date. Congrats, boys!"

Cam and Royce clinked bottles together and took simultaneous celebratory gulps. It felt like half the town had packed into the brewery that day to cheer them on for all of Big Hops Brewery's newfound success.

Expansion—that was what today was all about. Lager of Love was a hit all across the states, and next week they would ship their first international orders. To the surprise of absolutely no one, Cam's ex-partner in the brewery had even called from Cabo to ask about the possibility of buying his way back in. To Cam's credit, he'd let Hank buy stock back into the place—at nearly five times the price per share that Hank had left at.

As for Royce and I? We were happy, healthy and still madly in love—which was good, because I was due to pop any day now. We'd spent the night before making gentle love to each other. In the hours after, just before we'd drifted off to sleep, Royce had held me, feeling the baby kick beneath his hand and going over our name options one last time.

"How's little baby Nicolette doing?" Royce asked, putting his arm around me as Cam moved through the crowd to mingle and get the party started.

"We're not calling her that." I laughed as I glanced at Nicky, who was pulling his alpha biker boyfriend over the bar for what was far from their first messy make-out session of the night. "Nicky will start thinking that we named her after him. It'll go right to his head."

"Aw, damn. Didn't think about that. What about … hmm. Can we give her one of those gender-neutral names? Aspen or Addison or, I don't know. Quinn or something?"

"Stop worrying about it." I moved my lips against his soothingly. "I have a feeling that when we see her, we'll know."

As it turned out, we were going to see her even earlier than we'd planned. The running pool at the Brewery was taking bets for guessing the time of birth, starting at midnight that night, and Royce had bought the very first slot.

When my water broke, and I started having contractions about halfway through the big party, right in the middle of Royce's toast, I had a feeling that he might have been right on the money.

"Okay, okay." Royce took a deep breath as he took my hands into his. "We've got our go bags in the trunk, and your birthing playlist on your phone. Anything else you need?"

"Only you, handsome." I was taking deep breaths too—out of absolute necessity. The contractions were already closing in, coming a little faster with every wave.

Dad had warned me that it would be a quick delivery, but even I hadn't expected it to all come together quite *this* quickly. I was grateful for Royce's hands on mine as the next round hit, only a few minutes after the last. "All I need now is you."

"A hospital might not be the worst idea, though." Dad threw Royce his keys and beamed with pride. "Meet you two there?"

Royce caught the keys and kept his arm around me, parting the crowd so we could get through the door. At this rate, I wasn't sure that I was even going to make it to the hospital—but Royce drove quickly and expertly, picking up a police escort from one of the alphas he'd befriended on the force since he'd moved here to Carter's Crossing on a more permanent basis.

A few months ago, we'd closed on a home of our very own. Royce had even helped me pick the paint for the nursery—though he'd left most of the painting to me and my artistic whims.

Our baby was born right at midnight that night. Dad had been right—I couldn't have asked for an easier labor. It was like my body had known exactly what it needed to do. After only a few hours of pushing, I was holding our baby girl firmly in my arms.

"She sure is sleeping a lot." Royce tucked one of his long, thick fingers in our baby's fist. She closed her tinier fingers around his digit, holding onto her alpha daddy like she already knew exactly who she was.

"She arrived so late at night," I pointed out. "Poor thing must be exhausted."

"Don't worry," the nurse cooed, coming in to take my vitals again. "She'll be up and wailing in a little while—and then you'll be kicking yourself for not enjoying the quiet more."

"Can I hold her?" Royce asked me, dropping his voice to a low whisper.

I nodded and passed her into Royce's arms. He was so big, our baby girl looked almost comically small cradled in the crook of his elbow. She only just barely stirred when we did the exchange, and immediately after, she curled back into Royce and went back to sleeping soundly.

"I'm impressed," the nurse remarked. "Looks like she might be an easy baby."

"She's a good girl," Royce agreed, cooing over her tiny swaddled face. "Isn't that right, Charlie? You're a good girl—beautiful and healthy and strong."

"Charlie, huh?" I smirked up at him as he bounced her gently. "That's … oddly perfect. Charlotte for a full name, maybe?"

"Charlotte Dana Wheeler." Royce nodded, pleased with himself for finally settling on something. "God, it all feels so real now."

"It hasn't felt real for the last nine months?" I accepted a cup of ice chips from our nurse and laughed. "It sure has for me, honey—she's been real for me since the moment we first knew she was ours."

"I think some small part of me has been waiting for the other shoe to fall," Royce admitted with a sigh. He sat down on the edge of the bed so he could cradle

Charlie between us. "But now … mm. Now I know that this is just how our lives are going to go. The three of us, together. Happily ever after and all."

"Just three of us?"

Royce looked down at me, a single dark eyebrow arching in amusement. "Wanting another one already, are you?"

"Guess I'm not quite ready to give up my paternity pants." I grinned. "You shouldn't have bought be such comfy ones if you didn't want them to get a little more use."

"We could be a family of four," Royce mused. "Just remember—you're the one who has to do all the heavy lifting."

"I haven't forgotten." I gave him a wicked look. "But I was thinking more like … five."

The nurse shot me a scandalized look. "Slow down there, daddies. You'll have to wait a few months. I'd recommend at least a year, in fact."

Royce pressed his lips to my forehead and settled his big, warm body snugly against mine. "I can wait," he assured me. "I'd wait ten years if I had to, you know."

"That might be a *little* much. You'll be fifty by then!"

"Guess it's a good thing I married such a handsome young thing, then." Royce's next kiss fell on my cheek, soft and loving. "It doesn't matter to me how long we wait, honey. We've got all the time in the world."

And we did. All my worries about the future had been assuaged completely. Being with Royce was like that now—he always had a plan for everything, and every single one of them involved the two of us working together to make our dreams come true.

Between running the diner together, managing the art and marketing at Big Hops, preparing our new home and being in love, we had plenty to keep us busy. Raising baby Charlie together—and all the other babies that I hoped we would raise after—would only add to all the joy in our lives.

When it came to our family, everything was a labor of love. It wasn't every day that two people found something like this—so warm and happy and full of care—but now that our happy ending was assured, I knew that we could take on anything life threw at us.

I smiled down at our baby again, seeing Royce's features in her dark eyebrows, and my own in her long, thick eyelashes.

Thank god for small miracles, right?

Made in United States
Orlando, FL
29 September 2023

37404005R00117